WHISKEY BLUES

BIJOU HUNTER

Publisher's Note: This is a work of fiction. Names, characters, places, and incidents are a product of the author's imagination. Locales and public names are sometimes used for atmosphere purposes. Any resemblance to actual people, living or dead, or to businesses, companies, events, institutions, or locales is completely coincidental.

Cover Design
Photo Source: Adobe Stock
Photographer: BlackDay
Cover Copyright © 2017 Bijou Hunter

Dedication
Sally, Mike, Jack, Max, and Luca for bringing light to a sometimes-dark world
Author Aimie Grey for putting up with my madness
Lovely Carina for being a Bijou encyclopedia
My betas Sarah, Janie, and Debbie for pointing out my blind spots
&
Judy's Proofreading

ONE - BONN

One misstep in life was all I needed to ruin everything. That's a fact no adult tells a kid. They promise everyone makes mistakes, and we can rebound from them. Maybe other people recover, but I've been stuck in a swamp of my misery for eight years with no one to blame except the asshole in the mirror.

I grew up with nothing much to hold onto. My father has too many bastard kids to keep track of, not that he ever tried. My mother suffered from alcoholism and reoccurring bouts of cancer until she became a shell of the vibrant woman she once was.

Though I'm not particularly smart, I was blessed with my parents' good looks and my father's athletic build. If my life goals were to be a slut like him, I'd never have any problem finding willing partners. Instead, all I wanted was Ruby Bauer, who I loved and lost because life doesn't provide a do-over button.

Time passed quickly after I lost Ruby. At first, anyway. Our daughter was born and took up most of my waking time. Those days, I worked in construction, barely making enough to pay for a bachelor-sized apartment.

I didn't push Ruby back then. Partly because I was too ashamed to share a room with her. But I also figured if I gave her space, she'd come around on her own.

Chevelle is now nearing her ninth birthday, and Ruby still hates breathing the same air as me. We have the most awkward parent-teacher conferences and throw separate birthday parties for our daughter. My waiting did nothing except allow us to fall into casual, lonely routines.

Ruby's tried dating, but her heart was never on board. I'd watch her with the guys and notice how fake her smile looked. As much as I hated knowing she was dating, I enjoyed seeing how little she liked the guys. Fortunately for everyone involved, she never went on second dates. No doubt, I'd have taken my stalking to a more dangerous level.

1

Ruby would have been pissed, and I hate when my woman yells at me.

So, I waited, thinking fate would bring us back together. Then, I waited, thinking I'd come up with the exact perfect way to win Ruby back. Then, I waited because I figured I was too stupid and unlucky to win her forgiveness.

Then one day, my cousin, Camden, said he'd married Ruby's little sister. Daisy went from hating him to wedded bliss because he refused to let her go. Camden chased and nagged and flirted and chased some more until she couldn't deny his charms. Now, they're living in the condo down the hall from me while I'm still alone every night.

So, no more waiting or expecting life to warm Ruby's heart. I'll have to do it the hard and ugly way. I won't give up until she finally sees me as a new man rather than the boy who broke her heart.

And my plan starts today.

TWO - RUBY

What's the statute of limitations on breaking a heart? Based on how people treat me, I'm the bad guy for holding a grudge against the man who broke mine. For them, a lover's betrayal is a petty crime, meaning the punishment shouldn't be drastic or permanent.

They tell me to date someone else. Falling in love and living well is the best revenge, they claim. Well, I live just fucking fine, but I have no interest in any other man. When the love of your life tears apart your dreams, what lower specimen will do?

Perhaps, I'm overly dramatic. Possibly, I hold grudges for longer than necessary. No doubt, I should have found a nice guy to help me forget about Bonn.

Perhaps possibly, no doubt, I don't give a crap what others expect from me.

My heart broke, and I'm unwilling to forget or forgive. I once believed Bonn was the best person in the world. Then, he crushed me. No way could I trust him or any man again. Screw them all. I'm happy man-less.

Besides, I've seen what love did for my mother. Sure, Sally got three kids out of her relationships, but she never found her true love. Or maybe she did, and he let her down like Bonn did me.

My mother and father met during her vacation in Jamaica. She longed for a wild adventure with a sexy man while he craved a green card. They lasted long enough for my birth and him to gain legal status. Once he left his opinionated wife, Dad created a new family with a woman who knew when to shut up and let the men do the talking.

Unlike my father, who wrote me off as part of his past, Bonn adores the little girl we created just out of high school. Chevelle is our angel, and we got lucky. Most girls in her class are "divas," which is a nice way of saying they're horrible bossy bitches.

Not our girl, though. Elle is well-behaved. When she wants to be bad, she doesn't throw a fit but instead gets sneaky. Elle is an ace at conning adults. I admit she's played me a few times with her big brown eyes and angelic smiles.

If not for our daughter, Bonn and I wouldn't see each other at all. I've done an exceptional job of avoiding him, even in the tight-knit Hickory Creek Township. Of course, Bonn helped by not forcing his presence on me.

Over the years, he did his thing while I did mine. We rarely spoke, managing to raise Elle together without sharing a room for more than a few minutes. Everything was perfect.

Now he's standing at my trailer door, holding a handful of purple flowers.

"How are you feeling?" Bonn asks, handing me the lavender and carnations.

"What are these for?"

"They're for you."

"I don't want them," I say, handing them back.

I catch a hint of uncertainty in Bonn's rich brown eyes. Rather than backing off, he smiles again and looks at Elle.

"Then, I guess Chevelle can have them."

Our daughter stops her homework long enough to beam at her father, adoring him in the way I once did. She trusts him completely. He's her frigging hero. I'd warn her about his ability to betray everything she believes in. Of course, I know Bonn won't hurt her like he did me. He's perfected the father role. Elle's his princess, and he'll die for her.

"Are we done?" I ask after handing the flowers to Elle and crossing my arms angrily.

"We're never done, Ruby."

Startled by his response, I stare at him for way too long. Bonn is as painfully handsome as ever, even just wearing a pair of faded blue jeans and a simple beige T-shirt. His dark hair is a little long and hangs over his brow. I fight the urge to reach out and brush it aside. Simply the thought of touching him after all this time sends my love-starved body into a damp whiny heat.

"What do you want now?" I ask after regaining my ability to speak.

4

Smiling in his breathtakingly beautiful way, he forces me to look away. Even after feeding my anger for all these years, I remain a slave to his brilliant smile. His power over me is why I avoid him.

"Why are you still here?" I ask when he only grins at me.

"Let's go to a movie together."

"Me too?" Elle immediately asks.

"Yeah," Bonn says, ruining my chance to shut down his crap. "We can see that movie you've been talking about."

I narrow my eyes, glaring hard at him. Meanwhile, Elle bounces joyfully at the idea of going out with both of her parents.

"Baby, go put your flowers in the vase," I say, buying a minute or two alone with Bonn.

Once she can't eavesdrop, I force Bonn off my trailer's porch and onto the dirt walkway. "What crap are you pulling?"

"A movie won't hurt."

"You purposely asked in front of Elle to force me to say yes."

"True."

"You're cheating. That's a scummy move I didn't expect from you."

Bonn's dark eyes scan my body before returning to my face. I still remember what that look means.

"If cheating is the only way to get what I want, I guess I'm a big fat cheater," he says, reaching out to touch my hair. When I dodge his fingers, he doesn't even hesitate before making another move. "Does this mean you agree to join us at the movies?"

After avoiding his fingers again, I'm snookered when he fakes me out with one hand and caresses my hair with the other.

"You're an ass," I grumble, "and cheating is your go-to move."

Ignoring my dig at his shady past, Bonn proudly smiles at how I allow him to touch a lock of my dark brown hair. "I'm taking that as a yes on the movie."

5

Elle watches us from the window, no doubt hoping he wins. I don't blame her, but Bonn's sneakiness still pisses me off. For eight years, he's respected my resentment toward him. We had an unspoken agreement to avoid each other, yet now he's eager to trash our truce.

Yeah, I'm more than pissed. I'm enraged and ready to lash out, but our kid is watching us with her big brown eyes. My righteous anger proves no match for my motherly love.

"When?" I say, already imagining how to avoid him while we share the same space for a few hours.

Bonn's arrogant grin is something I once adored. When he won a basketball game and flashed that smile, I melted into proud mush. I thought my man was so frigging flawless. Reality was a vicious bitch. I learned the hard way how Bonn is anything but perfect.

Today, he flashes me the same smile, and I only glare at him. I don't know what spurred his new pushy attitude, but I won't be his toy.

If he thinks I'm the same girl who loved him more than herself, he's in for a rude awakening.

THREE - BONN

I live on the opposite end of Hickory Creek Township from Ruby's trailer park. Arriving home at my condo, I sport a smile, some swagger, and a raging hard-on. Time has not stolen any of Ruby's exotic beauty, and I can still feel her soft, thick hair on my fingers.

Despite the anger in her dark eyes, I felt liberated by having her look at me. I've been a man lost in the dark for too long. As much as I love my daughter, Ruby is the only person whose smile can free me.

A year ago, I took a job as a stripper to make enough money to get the condo. I was sick of Chevelle visiting me in a dump, and my construction gigs never brought in enough regular income. I danced mostly at birthday and bachelorette parties in nearby Nashville. While I didn't enjoy getting pawed by drunk women, I was prouder than shit to be able to give my daughter a safe, attractive place to live.

Ruby never considers leaving her trailer park. She loves living at Lush Gardens with her family. It's the only home she's really known.

When her mother married a lawyer in town, they moved to a small house. Ruby told me how she never felt comfortable there, clearly realizing it was short term. The marriage didn't last, and she ended up back at the trailer park. At least, she got a sister out of the experience.

Up the elevator and down the tiled hallway, I'm nearly at my condo when Camden's twin brother, Dayton, appears from his place. The tatted biker wears only boxers that struggle to remain on his hips. I often think my cousin needs a woman to clean up his act. Or at the very least, someone to buy him new underwear.

"Long night?" I ask while he shuffles toward me.

"Drank too much shit. Got in a fight. Drank too much shit again. Banged three chicks and learned I can't handle that many holes at a time. A man has his limits, you know?" he says, rubbing his tired eyes. "Finished the night by drinking too much shit and eating four hamburgers. I think the fast food is what did me in."

"A normal person might think you were overcompensating for something."

"A normal person? Let me tell you a secret," he mumbles, leaning closer, so his shoulder-length blond hair falls into his face. "You are not normal, Bonn. Hearing that probably breaks your heart of gold, but you're all kinds of bad childhood fucked up."

"I'm not the one hungover at four in the afternoon."

"Yeah, but only because you're too stupid to know you're fucked. I understand my place in the world and embrace it."

"Uh-huh."

"Where you been?" he asks, grabbing a receipt hanging from my pocket. "Who'd you buy flowers for?"

"Ruby. We're going to the movies with Chevelle."

Dayton studies me with his dark eyes and then laughs loudly. "Like I said, you've got no idea how fucked you are. Good luck with that, buddy, and feel free to call me when you need to drown your sorrows."

After shuffling down the hallway, Dayton pounds on his brother's door until Camden answers.

"If I see your dick, I'm setting it on fire," Camden says, glancing down at Dayton's tattered boxers.

"Why are you always talking about my dick, man? It's weird."

Leaving the twins to bitch at each other, I head to my condo. Soon, I toss a beef patty in a frying pan and make a quick burger.

Once it's finished, I sit at my kitchen table and eat alone. Every day, I feel the ache of loneliness a bit more. I don't want to be the life of the party with a shitload of friends. I ought to be satisfied with Chevelle, the twins, and my mom.

But I want more.

Dating is pointless. Ruby is the only woman I could ever want. I miss her raspy laugh and how she bounces in her chair when she's telling a funny story. Today, I wanted so fucking badly to reach out and caress the curve of her full lips. My woman draws me to her without batting an eye, and no other chick will do.

Every night, she haunts my thoughts. I wonder how much she's changed since we were together. *Is she still the girl I loved all through high school?* Mostly, I wonder if she misses me.

Done guessing, I've forced my way back in her life, and I'm terrified.

This is my big chance to win back the only woman I'll ever want. All those nights imagining this moment, I'd focused so much on the part where we tried again that I never considered what would happen if our second chance crashed and burned.

Even worse, what if the people we are now don't click? *What if the Ruby I fell in love with as a teenager doesn't exist anymore?* Or what if I'd changed so much, she could never love me again?

My burger tastes bitter in my mouth, and I push away the plate. Sulking now, I imagine a life where my questions about Ruby aren't answered in the way I hoped. What kind of future can I have if she isn't the one for me?

FOUR - RUBY

I've lived in the Lush Gardens Trailer Park for most of my life, and I've never considered moving somewhere else. No apartment on my budget would provide two decent-sized bedrooms.

Lush Gardens is also where my family lives. Mom is a trailer down. My youngest sister, Harmony, and her son live next door. My other sister, Daisy, used to rent the trailer across from me.

Restless after Bonn's visit, I scrub the kitchen counter. I'm convinced if I clean the grout to perfection that my edginess will fade away. I'm wrong, of course. A spotless kitchen does nothing to alleviate the shock I feel since talking with him.

I need to talk to someone, but Daisy is too over the moon in love to understand my unwillingness to dive headfirst into romance. My mother tends to think the impulsive answer is always the correct one. Harmony is my only hope for a decent pep talk. I text her at work to see if she'll drop by my place once she's home.

In the living room, Elle keeps rearranging the bouquet in the vase, wanting them perfect. I watch my daughter marvel at the mix of purple flowers. She fixes them, sits back to admire her work, and then plays with them again.

"Why are you so excited?" I ask, hearing too much crankiness in my voice. "Your dad has given you flowers before."

"Yeah, but he never gave you any," she says without looking at me.

I don't answer. What's there to say to a starry-eyed child? Elle loves her daddy, and he's simply crazy about her. Admittedly, I've always been a little jealous of their relationship.

My father never wanted me. When I was little, he humored me out of pity. Then, once he could stop taking my calls, the man jumped at the chance. He had a family he loved, and I wasn't part of it. I'd been the side effect of a marriage of convenience.

Bonn isn't like any of the fathers I've known. Whenever I see divorced or single dads with their kids on the weekends, they seem a bit off-kilter and spend a lot of time checking their phones. No doubt they love their kids but don't know how to relate to them.

Bonn doesn't suffer from part-time dad syndrome. He and Elle love spending every weekend together. They go to the movies, play games, and goof off. He's the best damn dad he can be, which says a lot considering his father is an asshole who ignored him worse than mine did me.

I rarely let myself imagine what life could have been like if Bonn hadn't cheated with Kim Crawley at a house party. The fantasy is too powerful and breaks my heart each time the dream lingers. I'd loved him so much, and we made a beautiful child together. If he hadn't cheated, we'd probably have another kid or two. We'd live in a house with a yard and maybe even have a dog.

Elle is still arranging the flowers when Harmony knocks on my door. My blonde sister enters with her three-year-old son, Keanu, resting on her hip. Our gazes meet, and she knows I need to bitch privately.

"Betty needs you," Harmony tells Elle, mentioning our mother's best friend. "She's washing her dog, and you know how the bugger likes to run."

My girl smiles immediately and wiggles into her flip-flops. Harmony walks down a few trailers and drops off the kids with Betty. Returning alone, she switches on her phone to the 1980s pop, knowing I need decent tunes to help with my moping.

"What happened?" she asks, sitting on the couch and reaching for me.

I cuddle under her embrace, soaking in her pampering. "Bonn showed up with flowers and guilted me into going to a movie with him."

"Guilted you how?"

"He asked in front of Elle. If I said no, I'd be the bad guy. Why in the heck should I always be the tough parent?"

11

"Because he's the part-time one."

"Yeah, while I'm the one with homework duty and all the boring stuff," I grumble.

"Do you want to go to the movies with him?"

"No."

"Are you sure?"

I look up at Harmony's pretty face and give her my ugliest scowl. "Why would I want to go to the movies with that cheating dickface-asshole-stank loser?"

"Well, he's a sexy, cheating dickface-asshole-stank loser."

Grinning, I nuzzle my head against her shoulder. "That's true, but he's the scum of the earth. The worst of the worst."

"So very true."

"I hate him."

"I know."

"He broke my heart, and I hope his dick falls off."

"It no doubt will."

My thoughts return to the time I shaved Bonn after he'd gotten into a fight with some fool making eyes at me. With his busted knuckles, he couldn't clean himself up to go to church with his mom.

Holding the razor, my fingers shook. I feared I'd cut off his pretty face. He only laughed and teased me for being shallow. If I loved him, his lack of a face shouldn't matter. I laughed, too, until I cut his chin. Somehow, my mistake made us laugh harder. Like most young people in love, we were so fucking stupid.

"I miss him," I admit to Harmony. "Even after all these years, I can't pretend he wasn't the one."

"I know."

"I'm afraid to go to the movies and have him hurt me again."

"I know."

"I'm happy without him. If we spend time together, he'll remind me of what I lost. Then, I won't be happy. It's like he wants to hurt me again."

"I know, but maybe he only wants to be friends with his baby mama."

Rolling my eyes, I hate that term. "I don't want to be friends with Bonn."

"In high school, he was your best friend. Was all that just the sex?"

"No," I say, letting myself remember the sex for a second before squashing the memory.

"Then why can't you be friends now? No sex or romance. I'd want to be friends with someone who shared a kid with me and has an appreciation for 1980s classics."

"He does have good taste in music."

"And he loves Elle."

Sitting upright on the couch, I frown so much I hurt my face a little. "She'll think we're getting back together if I spend time with Bonn."

"Life is full of disappointments. Elle's still a lucky frigging kid to have two parents who love her so much. We had to make do with one parent and her wacky friends."

I think of my mother, Sally, and her besties, Betty and Charlie. The women were tight in a way I never could be with anyone except my sisters.

"I miss Daisy," I mutter while rubbing my gut and wondering if I've gained weight. "I kinda hate Camden for taking her away."

"I totally hate him, but can you blame her for wanting his sexy loving? I mean, we're great, but I don't look nearly as good with my shirt off."

No doubt, a lot of people would rejoice at the thought of my beautiful sister shirtless. Camden's twin brother, Dayton, might even start a standing ovation.

"If the movie with Bonn goes badly, will you join me for wallowing in self-pity ice cream?"

"Even if it goes well, I'll never say no to ice cream. In fact, I could go for some right now."

"Can you stay for dinner?" I ask, putting my diet ideas on the back burner.

Harmony walks to the fridge, where she rummages around for sweets. Finding nothing fattening, she frowns at me.

"You make dinner, and I'll get us a decent dessert."

Knowing Harmony will be around to cheer me up tonight, I shrug off my bad mood. A movie with Bonn will only be as painful as I make it. He isn't a bad man in most ways. Unfaithful, yes, but he won't hurt me in an obvious way.

And Bonn fucking someone else is no longer my problem.

FIVE - BONN

Ruby opens the trailer door wearing ragged beige jeans and a pale gray shirt. She thinks this outfit will turn me off and prove her indifference.

Unfortunately for her big play, even in a gunny sack, she's a vision of beauty. I reach out and caress a lock of her straight, dark hair hanging from a messy ponytail. Ruby doesn't pull away. She only stares blankly at me, going all-in on her lack of interest ploy.

"I brought new flowers," I say, lifting them for her to see.

"I don't need more flowers."

"You can never have enough beauty in your life."

Ruby takes the mixed bouquet and smells the flowers. "That's true, but I'd hate for you to spend all your stripper tips on me."

Her dig hits me in the gut just like she hopes. Ruby knows I want to keep my stripper job a secret. Unfortunately, a bitch from high school hired me for her bachelorette party and invited Ruby. No one in Hickory Creek Township can mind their own damn business.

"I work hard for those tips, so I'll decide how I spend them," I mutter, frustrated by how Ruby won't give an inch.

With her lips twitching, Ruby wants to smile at my irritation. I study her luscious mouth, remembering the way it felt against mine. Ruby was a great kisser. Even only sampling two other girls—one of them was sloppy drunk—I'm still certain Ruby possesses a natural talent. When her lips were on mine, I became her slave.

No longer irritated, I smile at the thought of kissing Ruby again. Her dark eyes lose their amusement as she notices my change in demeanor.

"Why are you doing this?" she asks in a low, frustrated voice.

Before I answer, Chevelle appears from behind her mother. My little girl smiles in a way that makes me feel like a million bucks. Though fatherhood scared the hell out of me when I found out Ruby was pregnant, Chevelle made the job easy.

"Are you two ladies ready to go?"

While Chevelle quickly nods, Ruby only stares at me. She's dying to know why I'm pushing her now. Knowing nothing I say will soothe her anger, I take our daughter's hand and walk to my SUV.

Once in the back seat, Chevelle keeps a smile plastered on her lovely little face. A scowling Ruby sits next to her, though I spot her smile when Billy Idol plays on the radio.

We both had a thing for 1980s music. In high school, when everyone was listening to the current fad, our tastes tilted toward an awkward era of big hair and synthesizers. I still think we were the coolest kids at Hickory Creek Township High School.

Tonight, when our gazes meet in the rearview, Ruby shoots me a dirty look. She's pissed, and I'm unsure how to soothe her anger. We rarely fought back when she was mine. Our relationship was so easygoing that people often mocked our happiness.

The theater isn't busy on this weekday evening. Chevelle doesn't like crowds and is easily intimidated by rude people. I don't know how she survives life in the Lush Gardens Trailer Park. No doubt, having so many ballsy women around keeps her safe.

Once I pay for the tickets, we wait in the short concession stand line. My gaze notices how her ragged jeans do nothing to hide her curvy butt and hips. I study her figure, spotting a bit of her white bra where her shirt collar falls to the side.

With only my hand as company for so many years, I don't need much stimuli from this particular woman to make me wish I'd worn a different pair of jeans.

Getting dressed earlier, I thought I was fucking brilliant to choose pants that hugged my ass. Ruby once said she could play the bongos on my butt, and I wanted to remind her of what she was missing.

Except now, my jeans are way too damn tight for the boner I'm sporting. Making matters worse, Ruby reaches up to fix her hair, and I notice the flesh between her shirt and pants. Now I'm wondering if I can jack off in the bathroom without alerting the entire theater.

Chevelle takes my hand as we wait in line for snacks. Her childlike glee puts a cold rag on my hot dick. I regain control of myself just in time to see Ruby's side glance straight out of a men's magazine. Her dark eyes shimmer and her frowning lips are never more kissable.

This woman's got me so wound up that I'm relieved Chevelle is around to play cockblocker. Without her, I'd soon be humping Ruby's leg.

SIX - RUBY

Once the movie starts, Elle loses interest in everything except what's happening onscreen. Bonn is the complete opposite. As soon as the trailers are over and his daughter's attention is elsewhere, he focuses solely on me.

I force my gaze to remain on the screen and ignore his attention. Bonn's hickory-colored eyes were once hypnotic, drawing me to him. We were obnoxiously in love once, and I fear believing we can be that way again.

Unable to stop myself, I peek at Bonn to see if he's still watching me. When I find him staring, I wind up my courage and glare hard. I want him to feel awkward about his behavior or bothered by my anger. Instead, the jackass smiles at me.

Worse still, I return his smile without thinking. Bonn's hypnotic eyes con me again. Even after I look away, I remain under his spell.

The movie drags on while I stare at the head of the lady sitting in front of me. I can't even look at Elle without worrying I'll catch Bonn's gaze.

Halfway through the movie, I swear Bonn moves closer. Even with our daughter playing buffer, I'm aware of his every movement for the next hour.

All smiles by the credits, Elle turns to me and asks if I liked the movie. I nod, even though I can't tell her a single thing that happened. My baby beams at Bonn and asks if he liked the movie, too.

He also nods but doesn't give details about the plot. I nearly smile at the thought of him feeling half as lost as I do. Aren't we foolish to long for each other after so many years? Life never offers second chances to people like us. We had our shot and failed.

Sufficiently irritated again, I'm ready for our pizza dinner. No more longing glances or wistful memories.

Entering the restaurant, I'm ready to show Bonn where I stand with his sudden interest. Then, I catch a glimpse of us in a nearby mirror, and my sense of righteousness deflates. I'm gutted by the sight of the family we could have been.

"What's wrong, Mom?" Elle asks.

"Nothing," I lie, still sulking while staring at the menu.

I can't let go of the image of what Bonn, Elle, and I could have been if he hadn't screwed up. Would we have had another kid by now? Where would we live? I know now that he only affords his apartment because of the stripping money. If we were together, he'd never even consider the job. Would we be cozy in a trailer at Lush Gardens?

"Ruby," Bonn says, startling me from my thoughts. "Ready to order?"

Elle frowns at me, probably worried I'll ruin her good time. She's always wanted us to spend time together. I know she's heard stories about Bonn and me from high school. In her innocent mind, she thinks we should be a fairy tale with everyone living happily ever after. *Doesn't love conquer all, including a hero who can't keep his dick in check?*

I order a pizza slice and try to focus on Elle. She's a huge fan of Dolly Parton's music and wants to write a school report on her, but the teacher said she couldn't. Elle doesn't understand why Dolly can't be her hero. I don't have the heart to tell her it's because the teacher wants her to pick someone more befitting of one of the few multiracial girls in school.

"How about Charley Pride?" Bonn suggests, having figured out what I did. "I think the teacher wants you to have a hero who's a person of color."

"Why?"

"Because your teacher is from a small town and thinks that's how life works," I mutter, pulling off the pepperoni and making a cheese pizza.

Elle frowns at me and then Bonn. "I don't get it."

"Charley Pride sang at the Grand Ole Opry," Bonn offers.

"But I want to do Dolly Parton."

"School is about conforming," Bonn explains without skipping a beat. "When you're older, you can write about anyone you want. While you're in school, you do what the

19

grownups say. I had to do that, and Mom had to do that. Now, we're grown up and can do whatever we want."

"I want to be grown up," Elle says, giving a dramatic sigh.

"Being an adult is pretty boring," I tell her.

Elle looks at Bonn and then at me. Nodding simultaneously, we confirm the boring adulthood idea. Torn between doing what she wants and having fun, Elle sighs again.

"Can I see your phone?" she asks me.

Once I hand it to her, she searches for information on Charley Pride. Whatever she finds soothes her bad mood.

"He played baseball," Elle says, already wanting to write her paper.

I study Bonn, impressed by his ability to make Elle feel better. Even knowing he's a great dad, I've rarely watched him with her. For whatever reason, I'm in a worse mood after witnessing his skills. I'm probably jealous of how he sweet-talked her in a way I can't.

Or maybe a tiny part of me misses how Bonn used his smooth moves on me back when we were at our best.

SEVEN - BONN

After we return to Lush Gardens, Chevelle's long curls flutter in the wind. Ruby is forced to stand in front of her to block the harsh breeze. Laughing at how she can't see, Chevelle eventually digs her way out of her wild hair.

"I wish I had curls," Ruby says, smoothing aside our daughter's hair until we can find her face again.

"It's getting cold," Chevelle tells me. "Do you want to come inside?"

Even without looking at Ruby, I know she hates the suggestion. I'd love to spend more time with my two favorite girls but decide to think long term.

"Not tonight," I say, though the words burn in my throat.

Chevelle studies us, considering whether to make an issue out of my answer. She's desperate for us to be together, and my recent behavior has given ammunition to her dreams.

"Can we go to dinner again?" Chevelle asks Ruby.

"We'll see." Chevelle stares at Ruby with her big brown eyes until her mother relents. "Fine, maybe next week. Now go inside and get warmed up. I need to talk to your dad."

After giving me a tight hug, Chevelle heads into the trailer, where she turns on the TV and calls Harmony. I hear her on the phone and smile.

"She sounds like a teenager sometimes."

"I'm not ready for that," Ruby says, sounding tired.

Still smiling, I study Ruby's face and wish I could touch her lips. I don't know what she sees in my expression, but her gaze narrows.

"I'm not kissing you goodnight," she nearly growls.

"I wasn't asking."

I catch a hint of disappointment in Ruby's chestnut eyes. We both need a little more time together before we can end this evening.

So, before she walks inside, I lean forward. I don't kiss her as much as allow our lips to caress. Not even a taste, only a hint of what we might have again.

Ruby goes rigid, and I see surprise in her eyes first. That's followed by anger and finally feigned indifference. I know her well enough to understand how she can't allow me any power yet.

I hurt her, and Ruby's not good with pain. She's the tough sister, the one with more common sense and confidence than her younger siblings. Ruby can't fall apart, yet I make her feel like the world is spinning. I feel it spinning, too.

"Good night, Ruby."

"Uh-huh."

I stop and frown at her. "Wait, are you flirting with me?"

"What?" she asks, looking around like I'm nuts.

"The way you said uh-huh sounded seductive."

"No, it didn't."

"Oh, yeah, I get it. You're playing coy now. Okay, I see what you want. I'll talk to you tomorrow."

"No, not tomorrow. Why are we talking so much now?"

Fighting a smile, I ask, "Isn't that what you wanted? I mean, that's what you hinted you wanted earlier. I'm confused now."

"I haven't hinted at anything," she says, forcing her voice into an angry whisper rather than yelling. "What's wrong with you?"

Studying her, I know Ruby's pissed, but she's also curious. Not enough to overcome her bruised ego and a broken heart. No way can I expect her to come along willingly.

"I get it. You're not ready to admit anything," I say, taking a step back. "It's been a long time, and you're not ready to jump into anything. I catch you," I add before giving her a wink as if we're on the same page.

"Don't wink at me."

"You're right. We need to slow this down. I'll talk to you tomorrow, and we can make plans."

Ruby throws her hands up, storms inside, and slams the door on me.

Despite her anger, I walk back to my car, feeling like a king. I know Ruby, and she'll answer when I call tomorrow. No doubt, she'll give me a ton of grief I deserve. If we had gone through this crap years ago, we'd be together now.

Instead, we avoided making things ugly and prolonged the inevitable. The time for hiding is over, and I'm ready to tear open the wounds to see what we have festering inside.

EIGHT - RUBY

Salome "Sally" Slater arrived in the US at the naïve age of 17, knowing very little English and having few skills. From nanny and maid, she eventually got her high school equivalency and started waitressing. When she saw the chance to try out a manager position at the diner she'd worked at, Sally jumped at the opportunity.

My mother is a solid mix of spontaneous wild woman and simple country girl. She grew up on a farm, having small dreams. Now, she lives in a trailer park and enjoys a solid job. If not for her love of liquor and pretty men, she'd be an average middle-aged woman unwilling to rock the boat.

Today, Sally and I wait in a coffee shop. I suspect her mind is on that boat and whether she can go against her nature to play life safe when it comes to a paycheck.

"I don't know what they want. We shouldn't assume anything," Sally says to me as we wait.

"I'm here for moral support. I make no judgments," I reply, yawning after another restless night thinking about Bonn.

"While we're waiting, do you want to talk about your date with you know who?"

My mother has a way of pinpointing my weaknesses and diving in. I've been in a state of confusion, and quite frankly heat, since our night at the movies. Since then, Bonn has taken to texting me happy messages such as "thinking of you" and "I miss you." I never reply, but I still reread them a dozen times an hour. Bonn's driving me crazy, and I haven't even seen him in days. What the hell will happen when we're face to face again?

"It wasn't a date. The only good thing to come out of that night was he said I could use his laundry room if I wanted."

"He's still so handsome. Very polite, too. Did I tell you he said I looked beautiful last Halloween?"

"Yes, you've told me that story about a dozen times. Now, let's sit here silently and wait for the Hallstead women to drop their bomb."

My mother grins at my bad mood, and the woman has a great smile. Her personality is why she succeeded even when life wasn't helpful.

She's right to be wary of the Hallstead family who runs Hickory Creek Township. Except since Daisy married Camden, Sally and his mother, Clara Hallstead, have bonded over talk of future grandchildren. That doesn't mean this secret meeting wasn't an odd request.

Clara enters the small diner, wearing all black as if she's in mourning.

"She's dressed for a heist," Sally whispers to me.

Blonde hair wrapped into a perfectly styled messy bun, Clara smiles at us with her red painted lips. She's joined by the town's mayor, Eloise Hallstead, who's wearing all white to her sister's black ensemble.

"You brought Ruby," Clara says. Despite her casual tone, I feel singled out. "Good. She has experience with restaurants."

Once the Hallstead women sit across from us with their fresh coffee, Sally asks why we're here.

"See that burned-out lot?" Clara asks, gesturing across the street to where De Campo's Pizza Shop stood before a fire destroyed the business.

"Yes, so?" Sally asks.

"The owner, Mickey, received pressure from the Brotherhood to sell his place. They planned to switch it out to a strip club. I requested Camden ask his father to back off. Mojo agreed, and the issue was settled."

"Then, someone burned down the place," I say, knowing everyone suspected Bonn's long lost half-brother, JJ.

"Yes. Mickey knows the Brotherhood will never let him be, so he's prepared to sell the place and move on."

"What does that have to do with us?"

"My sisters and I purchased the lot from Mickey, intending to reopen the restaurant. We'd like to hire you as a consultant during the building process and then as a manager once it opens."

"What sort of restaurant?"

"We plan to stick with Italian. De Campo's chef remains, and he prefers to do more than bake pizzas."

"If the Brotherhood wants that lot, won't they get it from you the same way they got it from Mickey?" I ask, choosing my words carefully.

Clara glances at her older sister and then smiles at me. "We don't suspect a restaurant owned by the sheriff and mayor will suffer similar issues."

"How soon will you start rebuilding?"

Eloise finally speaks up. "We're currently pushing through the title change and city planning requirements. Clara's hired a contractor to oversee the project. We see a start date in the middle of next week."

"What do you need me to do?" Mom asks.

"Help us work on menus. The chef has a million ideas, but we know that's a mistake. We need you to help us hire new staff since many are afraid to work there now."

"But they shouldn't be afraid, right?" I ask, unsure why the Hallstead women would challenge the Brotherhood over a pizza joint.

"No," Eloise grunts as if I've challenged her.

"I like the idea of working on this project," Sally says. "But I don't want to get between you and the Brotherhood."

"They'll do nothing because they can do nothing," Clara says, sounding friendlier than our distinguished mayor.

"What the hell?" Sally says, shrugging and smiling at me. "I'm a big fan of girl power, so I'll help out and divide my time between Applebee's and your place."

"We'll expect you to more than help once we open. You'll need to quit your current position and come on full time at our restaurant."

"We can talk about that when the time comes."

Eloise and Clara want my mother to bow to their will. Most people in Hickory Creek can't fall to their knees fast enough for the Hallstead family, but Sally Slater's one fault is her temper. She can't have anyone putting her into a corner without her ego forcing her to punch her way out.

"We don't like leaving open the door to problems," Eloise tells Sally.

"You're offering this to me because I am Daisy's mom. You also know I fooled around with Mojo years ago. This entire thing is a power play against him and the Brotherhood. I don't mind any of that because those boys like to cheat. Why shouldn't you play dirty too? No, I don't mind you using me to make a point to them, but I won't sign off on a future job when I have bills to pay now."

"You don't trust us?" Clara asks, feigning shock.

"Would you if the roles were reversed?"

"Not even a little."

"Well, then we understand each other. I will work hard for your restaurant when the time comes."

"How about you?" Eloise asks me. "Would you like a job?"

"I wouldn't have to work the same shifts as my mother, would I?"

"What does that mean?" Sally grumbles.

"You're a hard-ass, and I prefer a less stressful work situation."

"Ungrateful," my mother sighs. "Work isn't meant to be stress-free. That's why it's called work, Ruby."

"Let's not have this conversation again," I tell her and then study the Hallstead sisters. "I don't know much about running a restaurant."

"You managed the Bend Over Bar in Common Bend," Clara says.

Ah, how much I miss my old bartending job at a strip club, complete with good tippers and few complaints. My current job involves considerably more whiners and a shit-ton more kids.

"I wasn't a real manager," I admit, still feeling nostalgic about the job I lost when the Common Bend sheriff went rogue.

"You have the experience, even if you lacked the title."

Giving a noncommittal nod, I'm nowhere near ready to quit a stable yet unfulfilling job for a position in the Hallstead family's vendetta project. Sally, Clara, and Eloise make small talk for another twenty minutes, mostly speculating how soon Camden and Daisy might have kids. Their friendly chitchat is a ruse between women with a long history of distrust. Despite their past problems, the new restaurant could offer my mother a real challenge in her otherwise rather sedate life.

NINE - BONN

I'm surprised when the woman running the party plays the Spanish version of Shakira's "Loco." Considering the party is full of bleached blonde girls from Tennessee State, I doubt any of them understands a single word of the song besides "loco," which they randomly yell out.

When I was ten, my mom enrolled me in dance classes to piss off my father. Of course, Jude "Howler" Hallstead never cared enough about my existence to feel anything at all.

As the only boy in class, the instructor treated me like a prince while the girls were gentle compared to what I was used to in my neighborhood. All my life, I got mocked for being a pretty boy. But in class, my good looks made me one of the girls.

Tonight, my looks make me a wiggling chunk of beefcake for squealing girls barely old enough to legally drink. I don't hate the job because I know how to focus my mind elsewhere. If I let myself feel their fingers on my body or listen to their obscene offers, I'd likely go nuts.

The one stripper from the agency I've spoken to is a stoner who dances to keep himself in pot and munchies. Jeffrey is never sober enough to care one way or another about the women around him. He hinted more than once how women don't do anything for him. However, his body sure does something for them.

"I'm selling the fantasy of a man at their disposal," he told me. "Besides, dancing is good exercise, and I eat too many chips."

I wish I could shrug off the gross factor as easily as Jeffrey. I'm sure other strippers even enjoy the attention. For me, I get through the parties by thinking of Chevelle and Ruby. No matter what the women scream or how many yank at my pants to give me a tip, my mind remains locked on my dream of living as a family.

In my fantasy, the house we live in changes. Sometimes, we have pets. Other times, I imagine a second child. I see us during the holidays. I have a hundred different fantasies to distract me through each night of stripping.

The worst part of every job is returning to my condo and cleaning up. My mind can't latch onto a fantasy. Instead, I'm forced to think about how long I have left with this job. At twenty-six, I could probably get away with dancing for another few years. Eventually, time will catch up with me.

What then? I lack the kind of skills to make a good living. Even with the money from stripping, I sweat each bill. I skip lunches, walk rather than drive, and keep the lights and TV off whenever Chevelle isn't visiting.

Even saving as much money as I can each month, I'm only biding my time. And what if Ruby gives me another chance? I'll have to quit dancing, leaving me stuck with the seasonal construction work that left me broke only a year ago.

If I want to improve my financial situation, I need to do something big. Though I have something in mind, the idea could easily end with me crashing and burning.

TEN - RUBY

Elle opens the door to her father's condo and walks inside with the air of a girl used to such posh surroundings. I can't deny the place is a million times fancier than our trailer. The ceilings are high, and everything shines from the wood floors to the granite countertops. I stand in the doorway and accept how stripping has been good for Bonn. The condo looks like something I'd see on HGTV.

"Mom, come inside," Elle says, opening the large stainless-steel fridge. "I'll get you a drink."

"I'm good."

"Dad goes to the store on Wednesdays. He has a lot of stuff now."

I don't argue with Elle, who wants to show off. She brings me a soda and uses a step stool to climb to reach the crackers. Once she's gotten enough snacks, she turns on the large flat screen on the wall.

"Want to watch TV?" she asks.

"I'm here to use the laundry, not hang out," I say, hating how my body reacts to the faint scent of Bonn's aftershave.

Nodding, Elle hurries to show off the small laundry room with a brand-new washer and dryer.

"Dad puts the cleaning stuff up there," she says, pointing. "I help him wash bedding sometimes."

Imagining Bonn and Elle together always tears at my heart. He's so good with her, just like I knew he'd be. When I got pregnant, I dreamed of the moment I'd first see him holding our baby. I never got to enjoy that milestone or a million others. Even after all these years, I still want to cry my eyes out when I think too long about what we lost.

"Are you okay?" Elle asks, taking my hand in hers.

"Yeah. I think I'm about to start my period."

Elle's grown up surrounded by women and is well versed in the struggle between female hormones and sanity.

After putting on a load of laundry, I walk with Elle to the living room, where we work on her school assignments.

She struggles with math as usual but blows through the writing and reading stuff.

"Dad said you tutored him with math," Elle shares later while leaning against me on the large couch.

"Yeah, he didn't get a lot of stuff at first. He'd fallen behind, and your dad doesn't like to ask for help. Grandma Franny isn't good at math and couldn't help him. Once I tutored him a little, he got the hang of it and is good at math now."

"I hate math."

"Because it's hard. Once you catch on, it won't be hard, and you won't hate it."

"Do you like math?"

"No, but I don't hate it, either."

"Do you hate Dad?"

Frowning, I exhale hard. "No. Why would you ask that?"

"You never want to talk to him or see him."

Avoiding her gaze, I nearly whisper, "Your dad and I aren't friends anymore."

"Why?"

"It's not something you can understand."

"Why?"

"Because you're eight. When I was eight, I didn't understand things, either. But I knew my mom and dad loved me."

I hate lying to Elle, but she doesn't need to know her grandfathers are assholes. When she's older, she can hear the truth without it defining her.

"I wish you and Dad were together."

"I know."

"We could live with him."

"Elle…"

"Isn't it okay for me to want that?" she asks, staring at me with her beautiful brown eyes.

"You can want whatever you want, baby. What you need to understand is how much your dad and I love you. How you're the most important person in our lives, and we'll always support you."

32

Elle leans over and wipes a tear from my cheek. "Do you miss Dad?"

"No."

"It's okay if you do. He misses you too."

"Did he tell you that?" I ask, hating how interested I sound.

"No, but he talks about you a lot. That means he misses you. Like how Aunt Harmony talks about Aunt Daisy a lot because she misses her. That's how come I talk about Aunt Daisy's cats because I miss them and wish we could have a cat."

"Maybe we can get one for your birthday."

"Really?" she asks, her eyes lighting up.

I feel like an asshole for distracting her with a pet, but I can't deal with her questions about Bonn. This condo is his, and everything inside reminds me of what I lost. Hell, even my baby's sweet smile is a kick to the heart.

Nearly an hour later, Bonn enters the condo and is greeted by Elle announcing how we might get a cat. He smiles at her news and then takes in the sight of me. I try not to care what I look like. Of course, I couldn't help putting a little more effort today into my appearance than during movie night.

"I like your braids," Bonn says, lightly tugging at my hair.

"The laundry's almost done."

"You want to stay for dinner?"

"No."

"Please, Mom," Elle whines, killing my resolve with her desperation.

"Fine, but I need to talk to your dad alone for a minute."

Elle dances around, excited about staying for dinner and her future cat. I hear her dialing my phone to call Harmony.

"I want to name him Pepper," Elle tells my sister.

Bonn and I walk into the laundry room, where the dryer quietly rumbles.

"What's up?" he asks, full of innocence.

"Did you say I could use your laundry, so I'd feel bad that I can't give Elle all this?" I ask, waving my hand angrily and fighting the urge to slap his perfect face. "Did you want to rub things in, and let me know how well you're doing with your stripper cash?"

"Whoa, hold up. I know you're nursing a sizable grudge against me, but you can't possibly be angry enough to seriously ask me that."

"Don't turn this around on me."

Bonn's a big guy, and the laundry room doesn't offer him much space. He's nearly on top of me, and I can't breathe with him so close.

"You know I want another chance for us to work. So, why would I do something to make you feel like shit?" he asks, playing with my braid again.

"I don't know why you do anything."

"Then, let me take you out to dinner so we can get reacquainted. That way, you'll know me better."

"No."

"Why?"

"I don't want to spend time with you," I say, sounding like a bratty kid.

"I don't believe that's true. Besides, we need to become at least friendly for Chevelle's sake."

"Friendly, huh?"

"Yes."

"I don't know if I can ever look at you without seeing Kim."

Bonn flinches ever so slightly at the mention of the bitch's name. He quickly rebounds and shrugs.

"Then see Kim, but we need to be able to sit down and have a civil conversation."

Crossing my arms, I wish I could look Bonn in the eye without wanting him to touch me. "We're having a civil conversation right now, and I don't want to see Kim."

"You see her around town anyway."

"Yeah, and she's fat and has horrible acne. Oh, and I hear her husband smacks her around. Hating the actual Kim isn't fun. Hating the Kim I see when I look at you is fun, and I don't think I want to give up that feeling."

34

"Well, if you like hating the Kim you see when you look at me, you should want to have dinner. It'll give you a chance to see that bitch Kim more."

"Crap. I walked into that one."

"Is that a yes for dinner?"

Rolling my eyes, I cross my arms tighter. "Do I have to be civil to you?"

"You don't have to do anything besides sit across from me and eat."

"You'll make me talk."

"No one is making you do anything."

Sighing, I mutter, "If it were only that simple."

"Nothing worth having is simple."

"A dinner between parents, not whatever we were."

"You know what we were, and I won't pretend I don't want you."

His honesty startles me, and my body already feels him again. Controlling myself, I shrug. "Fine, I'll go to dinner, but I can't promise I won't be rude the entire time. You bring out the worst in me."

Bonn's smile irritates me even more. He ought to fear my temper rather than find it sexy. The man refuses to be distracted from his current goal. However, I plan to wait him out.

Or maybe, just maybe, I might possibly find a way to push past my anger long enough to return to his arms.

ELEVEN - BONN

My mother claims she was born under a bad sign. Her parents were drunks who left her alone a lot. She had a learning disability that kept her from keeping up in class. Dropping out of high school left her with few work opportunities. All she had were her good looks, and she lost them after Howler Hallstead knocked her up.

Mom's been on disability for as long as I can remember. A coughing fit left her so lightheaded one day that she took a tumble down a flight of stairs and tore up her back and right leg. I was fourteen when she got hurt. While she was in the hospital, I stayed with Charlie Nestor and her husband, Billy, at the Lush Gardens Trailer Park.

At my lowest, I met the girl destined to change my life. I felt so comfortable at the trailer park that I hadn't wanted to move back with my mom. But she had no one else and needed me.

Alone now, Mom only leaves the apartment for doctor appointments and required evaluations by the Social Security Administration. I visit her a few times a week with groceries, and she watched Chevelle while I stripped. Otherwise, she's content with her TV.

I love my mom dearly, but walking into her apartment is like entering purgatory. Nothing about her or the place feels warm. All day staring at her TV and playing her online games, she takes no joy in anything. The only time she smiles is for Chevelle. She'll fake happiness for her granddaughter. Otherwise, she's waiting for death to take her.

"You seem chipper," Mom says, lighting a cigarette while I put away groceries in her tiny kitchen.

"Ruby and I are going out to dinner tomorrow."

"On a date?"

"Yes. I've made it my mission to win her back."

"Why now?"

"I'm sick of missing her."

"She'll never forgive you. Why waste time with someone who'll never give you what you want?"

"I love Ruby."

"You've barely spoken to her in years. If you didn't have Chevelle, you'd have forgotten about Ruby by now."

"That's your opinion."

Mom exhales hard, filling the air with smoke. "You've always been soft inside. When you were a little boy, I enjoyed your tenderness. Now, though, you're too old to have fairy tales in your head. You need to get serious about finding a woman who ain't holding a grudge."

"I am not soft. In fact, the easier thing would be walking away. Instead, I'm willing to suffer to reclaim Ruby. You don't have to agree with my thinking, but you could at least pretend to be supportive."

"Don't get your back up," Mom says, frowning at me in the poorly lit room. "I'm trying to help. If you don't want help, well, then okay. I'll just say good luck and leave it at that."

"Thank you."

"Just promise me if you give this a real shot, and it doesn't work out, that you'll finally walk away and find someone else."

"No," I reply, knowing no other woman can compare to Ruby.

"You don't want to end up alone like me."

"You made a choice, and I am, too. That's all we can do in life."

Mom gives me a harsh frown, revealing a rough, wrinkled face marred by years of suffering, illness, and negativity.

"I did the best I could."

"I know. Now, I'm doing my best."

Settling into her chair, Mom nods. "Just don't get stuck like I did after your father abandoned me. Don't focus on what you lost rather than searching for something new to hold onto. Can you do that, Bonn?"

"Yeah, Mom," I whisper, kissing the top of her head.

I don't point out to my mother how Howler never gave two shits about her while Ruby and I were once deeply in love. Comparing our situations makes no fucking sense, but I still pretend for her benefit. I can't stop being soft with Mom, but I'm done being a passive jerk when it comes to the rest of my life.

TWELVE - RUBY

Feeling a nervous wreck while preparing for my dinner with Bonn, I pray to the acne gods to keep my face blemish-free. Hair-wise, I'm relatively happy, but I can't deal with how fat my ass looks in these leggings.

"I need to change again," I tell my sisters sitting on my bed.

"No!" they cry in unison.

Daisy stands up and looks in my closet. "You've changed three times, but you always look essentially the same."

"What does that mean?"

"It means you only have two looks. Leggings with a long shirt. Or jeans and a long T-shirt."

"Why do you hide your butt?" Harmony asks, poking my rear with her bare toes.

Ignoring my youngest sister's question, I ask Daisy, "What else am I going to wear?"

"Why not show off your legs with a dress?" Daisy suggests.

"I haven't shaved this week."

"But you knew you were going on a date," Harmony says, stretching out on my bed. "Didn't you worry about getting naked with hairy legs?"

"I knew having hairy legs would keep me from doing anything stupid."

"With Bonn, you never know what could happen."

Daisy digs around in my closet before sighing dramatically. "You've gone a long time without sex. You might not make it to the restaurant before you use his leg as a stripper pole."

"Had to mention the stripper crap, didn't you?" I growl, thankful Elle is spending the evening at Sally's place.

"The man has a bod sexy enough for stripping. Yeah, I'm going to mention that when you claim you shouldn't hump him."

"I'm not a dog."

"Neither is he."

"Ugh, just help me pick something. Should I wear jeans?"

"No, you don't own a single pair that doesn't look beat to hell, and none of the holes are in the right places."

"Wear the dark green tunic," Harmony says, pointing at the closet. "It looks a little fancy, and the color makes your olive skin shine like the sun."

"Are you high?" Daisy asks Harmony.

"Just on life, sis."

"I forget how weird you are now that I've moved away."

"You live ten minutes from here," I point out.

"Feels like I'm in another state sometimes."

Before we get nostalgic, I find my two green tunics.

"Which one?" I ask Harmony while holding up the shirts I bought at Goodwill.

"The one on the left is lower cut. You'll show a little skin and make him want to see more."

"Since I'm not looking to seduce Bonn, I'll wear the other one."

Harmony loses her smile but doesn't complain. Daisy is too busy searching my closet for something better. I slide on the new shirt and check the long mirror on the back of my bedroom door.

"I look ready for a job interview."

"Nothing sexier," Daisy teases. "Doesn't matter what you wear. Bonn always looks at you like a starving man."

"He's an ass-face."

"Yes, but he's an ass-face who looks at you like a starving man."

"I can't forgive him, so this friendship thing is stupid," I mutter, crossing my arms.

Daisy hugs me and stares at our reflections in the mirror.

"You've never asked him why he did what he did."

"Who cares why he did it?"

"You do. I do. Harmony would if she wasn't dozing on your bed."

We glance at our sister and find her half asleep.

Smiling, I whisper, "She picked up some extra shifts to save up for Keanu's birthday."

"Well, then, we'll be quiet," Daisy says, taking my hand and tugging me from the bedroom. "I've been thinking about you and Bonn lately."

"Why is that?"

"My lunch period falls at a weird time, so I eat alone every day. I'm able to daydream a lot."

After wrapping my hair into a loose ponytail, I check my appearance in the bathroom mirror.

"Want to hear about my idea?" Daisy asks while standing too close behind me.

"I guess."

"You should ask him for the details about that night with Kim. Force him to own up to what he did. If you still want to punch his face, then nothing he does will ever change things."

"I don't want to know the details."

"Sure, you do. I know I would. Like did he always want Kim? Was it a coincidence they hooked up that night? Or was it something he had in mind for a while? That would tell you a lot more about Bonn than just knowing he cheated."

I think about her questions and how awful I feel hearing them. I don't know if I'm up to sitting across from Bonn while he shares the answers.

"He wants us to be friends. Well, I think he wants more, but he claims we should be friends. What if asking those questions makes it impossible for me to be his friend? Isn't that bad for Elle?"

"You've been angry for so long," Daisy says in her tender way. "Now, you have a chance to let go of the pain. I don't doubt it'll hurt more when you hear the words, but hearing them could help you heal. After all this time, don't you deserve a chance to move past what he did?"

"I never want to forgive him," I admit, seeing my frowning face in the mirror.

"Why?"

"Without my anger, I don't know who I am anymore. Especially when it comes to Bonn. My anger has defined our relationship for so long. Now, he wants to make things different, but I'm not ready to change."

"You've always been so strong, Ruby," Daisy says, hugging me from behind. "You can handle the truth. I'm not sure Bonn is strong enough to tell it. He's played the sad, nice guy crap for so long that I don't think he even understands why you hate him so much. Maybe it's time for him to face the truth."

I stand in my bathroom, feeling lost in a place I know with my eyes closed. Bonn stole many things from me years ago—trust, security, wide-eyed hope. No matter what I want to happen tonight, I don't know if I can ever reclaim what I lost.

THIRTEEN — BONN

The first time I saw Ruby, I was a goner. My teenage hormones went into overdrive, and I couldn't spit out a single sentence to her. Ruby assumed I was a rude asshole because I crazy-stared long after any normal person would have looked away. No matter her frowning face, I thought she was too beautiful to be real.

We became friends, but I had the worst crush on her. Whenever we shared a room, I felt like a damn pervert for hiding an erection. Ruby pretended to be indifferent to the opposite sex, and I almost believed her lies. That is until the day I got up the urge to kiss her.

My amateur attempt should have repelled Ruby. Instead, she pulled me closer and deepened the kiss. Turned out Ruby had a raging crush on me, too.

Those days are long past, and Ruby's loving feeling isn't something I can conceivably get back. Logically, I know I've lost her for good. *I just don't care.*

Ruby is everything I want, and I'd be a fool if I didn't win her back.

Answering the door, Ruby stares at me with dark, irritated eyes. I don't take her frowns personally. Anger makes sense to her for now. I need to earn my way back into her heart and bed.

"You look beautiful," I say once we're standing next to my SUV. "Green is a great color on you."

"I know."

Ruby's tone zaps away my confidence, but I regain it as soon as I'm sitting in the driver's seat. Her scent warms my SUV, reminding me of my end game.

"You're passing up a chance to mention how I clean up well. You know, and give me a dig about my stripping job."

Ruby glances at me before returning her anxious gaze to the front window.

"I'm not giving you a compliment," she mutters. "Not even a backhanded one."

"I understand. I've wronged you, and compliments are for good boys."

Ruby shoots me a pissed look, but I'm already laughing. She watches me chuckle and then slowly returns to her angry pose. I know she wants to smile. Ruby's always had a weakness for laughter. When others get started, she needs to join in.

Not tonight, though. Not after what I did to her.

FOURTEEN - RUBY

The restaurant reeks of burned onions. When my stomach responds by growling loudly, Bonn glances up from his menu and smiles at me. He looks so painfully perfect that I want to slap him. Why don't I beat the crap out of him until he looks like the rest of us lowly humans?

"Did you buy that blazer with your stripper cash?" I ask, deciding to take his earlier suggestion.

"No, my mom bought it for me for my last birthday."

Bonn's answer flows easily as if he expects my rude question. His confidence sends me into a rage, and I doubt I could hate him more right now. Well, I could find out he fucked Kim ten minutes before showing up at my place.

"Was Kim a good lay?" I ask as soon as the waitress leaves us alone in the nearly empty restaurant.

"Do you really want to know?" he asks, losing his casual smile.

"Let's rip open this wound and dig around in there."

Bonn leans back in his chair. "No, she wasn't. I wasn't any good, either. I was drunk and kept burping. I had nasty indigestion too and vomited in my mouth some. Do you want to hear more?"

"Sure, this is great shit."

Bonn plays with the fork for a second and then focuses on me. "Kim was wearing strong body lotion, and I licked it off her neck and started dry heaving. After that, I just laid there and let her do everything."

"Why pick Kim? Did you fantasize about her?"

"The only reason it was with Kim was that she was one of two girls flirting with me that night. The other was Sam Kendrick's ex-girlfriend. They broke up, and he told everyone their sex secrets. After that, every time I looked at Sera, I imagined Sam fisting her. With my stomach already upset, that image was too much. Kim was the only other option, and she made me think everything could be easy. I didn't have to worry about the future or responsibilities. I could be a poon-chasing eighteen-year-old without a care in the fucking world."

"Somehow, your story doesn't make me want to be friends with you."

"You asked."

"I thought the truth would be a good thing."

"In this case, the truth ain't pretty."

"So, you didn't like fucking Kim?"

"No. She had bony hips and a weird rhythm. I couldn't figure out what she wanted me to do."

"Did you have a thing for her before that night?"

"No, I told you. She was just available."

"Did you go to the party to fuck someone else?" I ask, fighting nausea rising in me. "Was that your plan?"

"No. I just wanted to let off some steam and let loose."

"What does that even mean?"

"It means I was tense and thought booze would distract me from that tension."

"Tense about what? About us having a baby or me being fat? What exactly was so bad that you needed to let loose?" I ask between clenched teeth.

"You don't really think it had anything to do with you gaining weight, do you?"

Nearly coming out of the seat, I lose my temper. "How would I know what goes through your fat head?"

"I was freaking out about being a dad," Bonn says in a stern voice. "You already felt like a mom because you could feel her inside you. You talked about Chevelle like she was real. But for me, she was still an idea until we had that last ultrasound. Then, I started freaking about how I was going to be a dad."

Adjusting in the chair, Bonn looks ready to bolt. We're both inching toward ending this dinner and going our separate ways. Fleeing would be easiest, but we keep our asses planted where they are.

"I didn't know how to be a father. I never had one. Neither did you. None of my friends had fathers around. I'd grown up without seeing how men were supposed to be with their kids. Even the twins didn't have a healthy relationship

46

with their dad. How would I do a good job? No, not even good. How would I keep from doing a shitty job with our kid when I didn't know what a good job looked like?"

Bonn sits up and again looks ready to leave. "I didn't know what to do. Chevelle was coming any day, and I felt trapped and scared. I was fucking losing it. The one person I normally talked to about stuff was the one person I couldn't tell how scared I was."

"I'd have listened."

"You were scared and about to give birth. I knew you'd think I was a fucking baby for whining."

"I wouldn't have thought that."

"I couldn't think straight. I needed space and to clear my head. I heard about that party, and I went and thought about how much I'd missed out on. I never partied. I never drank or dated anyone except you. I had stupid ideas in my head that made no sense the next day."

Bonn leans back in his chair and shakes his head. "Like, I couldn't see how I never partied because I didn't like partying. And I never drank because I'd seen how booze fucked with people. Or how I never dated anyone else because I'd never wanted anyone else. That night, I couldn't think straight. I could only remember how my dad didn't give a shit about his kids. How his dad hadn't given a shit about his kids. How I came from a long line of bad fathers. What if that crap was genetic, and I'd end up a bad father no matter what I did? I knew you'd stop loving me if I did wrong by Chevelle. I'd end up losing everything. So, I went to that party, looking for a distraction from my fear, and ended up losing everything anyway."

"Not everything," I mutter, hating to feel anything besides resentment toward him.

"Sure felt like it."

"Don't be so dramatic."

"You were my best friend."

"We barely spoke," I lie.

Bonn gives me a tiny smile. "You were also my lover, and my hand never picked up your skills."

"Well, I don't know what to say. Your hands were never lazy with me. Possibly, they were mad at you, too," I mumble, not wanting to find humor in the situation but enjoying the idea of Bonn suffering without me.

"No doubt. I lost their access to your body."

Sighing, I cross my arms. "We should stop kidding around before we pretend to be happier than we are."

"I'm not even a little happy."

"Me either. I've never felt more miserable."

Bonn studies my face. "I didn't think it was possible, but you grew up to be more beautiful than I could have dreamed."

"I was grown up back then."

"Not really."

"Just because you felt like a kid doesn't mean I did, too."

"Don't tell me you weren't scared out of your mind when you had Chevelle. That you didn't need your mom at your side to make you feel safe."

"I'm sure a lot of women feel like that with their first kid," I grumble, refusing to give him an inch.

"Wouldn't know about that."

"So, after freaking out about being a dad, you figured it out fine, anyway."

Bonn runs a hand through his dark hair, momentarily distracting me from my irritation. For a second, I recall how much I loved playing with his hair in bed. Refusing those thoughts, I wait for Bonn to say something. He watches me for nearly a minute as if knowing where my mind went.

"I thought fatherhood was hard, and some people weren't suited for it. But it's not. Being a father, a good one, I mean, is about making a choice. Do I choose to focus on the baby or the football game? Do I spend my extra cash on my kid or myself?"

"And you figured that out, when?"

"When I first held Chevelle," he says, smiling easily at the memory. "She was bigger than I imagined. Like the entire time you were pregnant, I pictured a tiny kitten-sized baby. I didn't know how I would hold something so small. I saw myself dropping her when she squirmed. But she wasn't that tiny. She didn't squirm the first few times I held her, either. She mainly slept, so that made her seem harmless."

I can't help smiling behind my hand at the thought of him fearing a defenseless baby.

"I was still scared when she cried. I remember the first time I had her alone with me for a few hours, and I knew she was going to cry. I kept waiting for her to wake up and wail. I didn't know what the hell I would do."

"What did you do?"

"I went through the checklist your mom gave us when you were pregnant. I changed Chevelle's diaper. I fed her next. I burped her. When she was still upset, I carried her around like a football to get pressure on her stomach. That was the magic move right there."

"Yeah, Elle had horrible reflux."

"After I survived her crying and puking and a cataclysmic diarrhea run, I figured the rest would be easy. Of course, they change their tricks as they get older, but I wasn't scared anymore."

"Just imagine how much easier it would have been if we did it together," I say, hiding none of my resentment.

"I imagine that daily."

Studying Bonn, I don't know what I feel anymore. "It was a mistake to start this conversation."

"It was going to happen eventually, so why not tonight?"

"Where can the conversation go after it's been focused on Kim's bony hips and Elle's dirty diapers?"

"We talk about normal things. Or we can return to discussing my one night with Kim. As long as you're sitting across from me, I'm happy."

"You have small dreams."

"Not really, but that's for another day."

"No, tell me now."

Bonn is saved when the waitress brings our overcooked food. She doesn't ask if we need anything before hurrying away to ignore her two other customers.

"This place sucks," I mutter, feeling hollowed out.

"Want to go somewhere else?"

Shaking my head, I sigh. "At least, it's quiet here."

After struggling to cut my chicken, I stick my fork in it and eat it like a shish kabob.

"I've had worse," I say, gnawing at the meat.

Giving me one of his brilliant smiles, Bonn does the same with his steak. Sensing our waitress isn't coming back, we steal a ketchup bottle from another table. Bonn walks to the kitchen when we need refills and requests the chef stop burning food long enough to fill our glasses. The entire dinner is a train wreck. Between talking about Kim and the shitty food, I should hate every minute. Instead, my face soon hurts from smiling so much.

FIFTEEN - BONN

As we return to Lush Gardens, Ruby fights to wear a frown like when I picked her up. Since her face won't cooperate, she covers her mouth the entire ride. Whether it was hashing out ugly shit or making the best out of a crap meal, Ruby's whole demeanor is lighter now.

Well, just until we stand outside her trailer and my fingers dance across her cheek. Ruby's gaze hardens first, followed almost immediately by the irritation spreading over her entire face.

"I'm gonna kiss you," I say.

"No, you're not."

"It's gonna happen."

"No," she growls, yet makes no move to flee into her trailer.

"I've wanted to kiss you for so long," I say, cupping her soft cheeks. "Now, you're standing here looking like the most kissable thing to ever exist. How do I say no to such temptation?"

"You try really, really, really hard."

"I remember when I *first* kissed you. I was such a frigging loser," I murmur as my thumb caresses her pouting lower lip. "I couldn't stop worrying about our teeth mashing together and knew you'd dump me if I knocked out your front tooth."

"You were such a loser," Ruby whispers, staring at me as if hypnotized. "I have every right to never forgive you."

"Forgiveness is for suckers and fools, and you're neither."

Despite my words and her nod, Ruby wants to forgive me. She dreams of something more. That's why she lets me kiss her.

I shouldn't dare to ask for more than a taste. I ought to control myself, but her flavor stirs up a million memories.

51

Long ago, I kissed this woman until we were out of breath yet hungry for more. *How can I stop when faced with someone so addictive?*

Ruby's hands get tangled in my shirt, forcing me closer. My fingers grip her cheeks, fighting the urge to explore her soft, dark hair.

My tongue meets hers, and she tastes like home. Wrapping her against me, I deepen the kiss. I need more. I hunger for everything that is Ruby.

"Knock it off," Ruby demands and shoves me away.

Despite her words and frown, I know she wants more, too. Her eyes devour me, remembering what happens when our bodies come together.

"Sorry, but you look great in green."

Ruby angrily wipes her mouth. "We had dinner and made peace. Now, we can co-parent. Nothing more than that."

"I'm going to win you back," I say, stating a fact.

"No, you aren't."

"I'll sweep you off your feet, and you'll forgive me because I'm so damn charming."

"How do you plan on doing that?" she asks, fumbling with her keys.

"It's a secret."

A trembling Ruby struggles to hide her smile. "You're making a mess of what should be a simple co-parenting plan."

"I already co-parent with you," I murmur, reaching out to touch her throat. "Now, I want to share a bed with you. I miss watching you sleep. And listening to you sing when you take a shower. I need to see you fight the urge to eat an entire pint of Haagen-Dazs. I want to watch bad TV with you and complain about how no one makes good music anymore."

Ruby stops trying to find her keys and stares at her door for a moment.

"You hate me right now," I say, softening my voice to almost a whisper. "But I want everything with you, and I won't give up until I have it."

52

Ruby turns her gaze toward me, and I can't tell what she's thinking. *Are my words romantic or ridiculous?*

"I have laundry to do," she finally says. "If I see you tomorrow at your place, so be it."

Locating her keys, Ruby can't take her eyes off me. I hold her gaze while she fumbles her way into the trailer. She shuts her door on me without saying another word.

I stand outside, waiting for her to peek out the curtains. First, she must argue with herself about not looking. Smiling at the thought of her internal battle, I wait and then wait a little bit longer.

Finally, Ruby appears at the curtains. Realizing I'm still standing there, she frowns, clearly flustered at my presence. I offer her a little wave before walking away. Ruby can't help watching me go and wonder what could have been. Especially when she still tastes me on her lips.

SIXTEEN - RUBY

I can hear Sally, Betty, and Charlie partying on the other side of the pond. They're enjoying mojitos and blackjack while I swing on the park's playset with Daisy and Harmony.

Elle and a local girl play dolls nearby. Not far away, Keanu jumps around, trying to catch bubbles that Charlie's husband, Billy, blows for the boy.

I hear my mom burst into laughter in the courtyard. Soon, Betty and Charlie hoot and holler. I don't know who won the poker game, but they're having a blast. With enough mojitos, those women will turn any occasion into a party.

"Bonn has it in his head for us to get back together," I say, rather than announcing I can barely sit after masturbating like a rabid sex-fiend all night to deal with a single super-hot kiss.

"No duh," Daisy says from the swing to my right. "He's been pulling the lovestruck act for years. About time he made an actual move."

"I don't know how I feel."

"You still care about him," Harmony says, digging her bare toes into the soft dirt under the swings. "A part of you has waited for him to man-up and reclaim you."

"I don't know if I want to be reclaimed."

"You're angry at Bonn, but you still want him," Harmony says, pointing out the obvious. "You should do a pro and con list to see if he's worth giving another chance."

"Okay, who wants to keep track of the pros?" I ask while they pull out their phones.

"I'll do pros," Daisy says. "I'm all about love and commitment and bowing to the will of a man's needs."

"Yes, we've noticed that."

Daisy bats her eyes. "I lost my self-control. Now, I need everyone else to be doomed to love like me."

"You're a virus desperate to infect," Harmony whispers. "Stay away from me."

"You love love."

"I do, but I don't want to be stupid in love. I'd like to be moderately intelligent in love."

"Lame. Okay, so, let's start with the pros," Daisy says.

"He's Elle's dad."

"He was your first love," Harmony adds.

Daisy nods. "He is really hot."

"He has good hygiene and keeps his place clean," I add, thinking about his pristine condo.

"If he's anal about that," Harmony says, "you might want to put it down as a con."

"He's normal about it. I guess, but I don't know. I mean, I don't know him anymore. He's a stranger. Maybe this was a bad idea."

"Moving on," Daisy says. "He's a good father and works hard to make Elle happy. I'd assume he'd do the same for you."

Harmony smiles. "He used to be romantic, too."

"Until he fucked someone else," I remind them.

"Yes, fucking someone else should definitely be on the con list."

Daisy jumps in with, "But he only fucked someone else once."

"Or so he claims," I mutter.

"Why lie all these years?"

"To make himself look good and make me look like the bitter bitch who hated him for one mistake."

"But Camden claims Bonn never screwed anyone else. Why would Bonn lie to Camden? You know men think so long without sex means his dick is defective."

"Maybe Camden lied to you to protect Bonn."

"Camden never lies to me!" Daisy cries, horrified by the very thought. We stare at her until she shrugs. "He doesn't share club business, which is fair. I don't tell him personal things about the students I work with. We keep our work lives separate, like so many other couples. We're so very normal that way."

I glance at Harmony, who rolls her eyes.

"Moving on," I sigh. "Okay, let's say he only cheated once."

"A lot of women would have forgiven him for one major screw-up," Harmony says. "Plenty of girls stay with cheaters."

"I refuse to swap fluids with other women. He's either mine or screw him to hell."

Harmony pats my knee. "And he knows that now."

"But what happens if we get back together and I gain weight again? You know how I chow down on Haagen-Dazs in the winter and pack extra pounds on my hips. Will the sight of me chunkier lead his dick to another girl?"

"Well, you said his freak out was because he was scared of being a dad, not because you were wonderfully round," Harmony says, and I smile at her wording. "Bonn knows how to be a dad now. He wouldn't freak out about another kid. Of course, maybe he lied about why he cheated."

"Maybe."

"Or," Daisy loudly interrupts, "maybe he finally got honest because you pushed for the truth. When he cheated, you shut down and kicked him to the curb. He never had to answer the questions before. I believe we should give Bonn the benefit of the doubt."

"You just want to double date," Harmony points out.

"Yes, but you just want her to stay so you'll have a single-gal buddy."

"I would never want Ruby to suffer just to make my life better."

"You're so full of it."

"So are you, but I was nice enough not to point fingers."

My sisters stand up and eye one another.

"Shut up, hippy," Daisy growls.

Harmony narrows her gaze. "Suck on a lemon, weirdo."

"Ladies, isn't it possible you're both wrong? It wouldn't be the first time."

"Hey, we're trying to help you!" Daisy cries, changing sides, so she's standing with Harmony now.

"I know, but I'm even more confused now."

Daisy grips my shoulders and stares into my eyes with her bright blue ones.

"Bonn is a good man worth giving another try. That's my opinion based on what Camden tells me, and I don't think Bonn would pretend to be celibate and hardworking for his cousin's sake. I believe he's grown up and wants to be the man you need."

Harmony nudges Daisy out of the way and takes my shoulders. "I agree with the weirdo. Yes, Bonn screwed up, and we'll never forget that. But this isn't about Bonn. This is about you being happy. He owns your heart and always will. If you see even the smallest shot of making things work, you need to take the chance."

"Well said, hippy."

I study my sisters and then blurt out what's been on my mind all day. "I'm so horny."

"Eww," Harmony says, stepping away.

Smiling sympathetically, Daisy nods. "We know, honey."

"I'm afraid I won't think straight with Bonn because I haven't had sex in so long. He was great in bed."

"Then, you need to fuck him and see if your brain works better," Daisy suggests.

"If I fuck him, I'll be stuck with him. Once I get a taste, I won't be able to walk away. The last time he broke my heart, I had a baby to distract me from the pain. What will divert my attention now that Elle is older?"

"If it comes to that, we'll keep you busy. I have a lot of laundry that needs doing," Harmony says.

Daisy nods. "I was thinking of painting one of the rooms at the condo. That should give you a few days of distraction."

"You two are just as sweet as anthrax-laced sugar."

"We'll hug the hell out of you if he hurts you again," Harmony promises.

"And I'll ask Camden to kick his ass, but in ways that won't show. We don't want Elle worrying over her dad."

I glance at my daughter playing. "She loves him so much. I never dreamed of living with my dad the way she

57

does with Bonn. Of course, my dad didn't love me like Bonn loves her. It's worth trying just to give Elle the family she dreams of."

"And the one you've dreamed of, too," Daisy says softly.

Smiling, I return to the swing. "Bonn still knows how to make my heart nearly rip itself free of my chest."

"Worry about satisfying your vagina first and let your heart figure things out later," Harmony says, swinging now too. "There's only so much a vibrator can accomplish."

Daisy sighs dramatically. "My poor sexless sisters."

"Camden has turned you into such an incorrigible slut."

"That he has, hippy."

Her newfound sluttiness aside, Daisy found her man and started a new life with him. I once had the same promise with Bonn. If we can put the past behind us, maybe Daisy's dream of double dates will come true.

SEVENTEEN - BONN

Everyone in North Tennessee knows more than a few rumors about Angus Hayes from the nearby town of White Horse. I've heard how he hides his victims' bodies under new construction. My mother once said he ate his enemies' hearts to gain their strength. She claimed he learned this practice while on a trip to South Africa.

None of the rumors interest me. The facts about Hayes are more impressive. He runs the town of White Horse without the help of organized muscle like a motorcycle club. He acts as a buffer between the Reapers club running Common Bend and the Serrated Brotherhood MC in Hickory Creek Township. A self-made crime boss, Hayes trusts no one.

Driving into White Horse, I arrive at his bunker-style office. An SUV sits in the lot, but I doubt it belongs to Hayes. A man his size would need more room.

Inside the office, I find a blonde woman sitting at a desk.

She looks up at me, yawns, and mumbles, "No soliciting."

"I made an appointment to meet with Hayes."

"I must have forgotten to write that down," she immediately replies. "Unfortunately, Hayes is booked all day."

"Can't you squeeze me in?"

"Why should I?" she asks, still staring at her computer.

"Well, you did lie about forgetting to write down the appointment. Seems like you could throw me a crumb as a way to make us even."

Her face scrunches into a surprised frown. "What makes you think I care if we're even?"

"One day, I'll work for Hayes, and you'll see me frequently. You seem like the kind of woman who wallows in guilt when she's wronged someone."

The woman's frown shifts into a grin. "I seem that way, huh? Well, that's why you shouldn't judge a book by its cover."

"I'll wait to see if he can give me five minutes."

"He won't."

Sitting nearby in the sparse waiting room, I take out my phone and work on a word search.

"I'd offer you coffee, but I don't want to get up for someone without an appointment," she says after a few minutes.

"I heard he married a woman named Cookie. Is that you?"

"Yep. I'm sweet as sugar, but he still won't see you."

"I'll wait and roll the dice."

"I already told you what happens."

Nodding, I return to the game on my phone. Thirty minutes pass before the front door opens, and Hayes stalks inside.

"Candy, get me a cup of coffee and take off your pants."

"We have a guest, and I'm not wearing pants."

Hayes doesn't glance at me. He's too busy admiring Candy's legs peeking out from her skirt.

"I don't remember you wearing that this morning."

"Age destroys the mind, boss."

Finally, Hayes turns to me and frowns. "Who the fuck are you?"

"Bonn Fletcher. We had an appointment, but our wires somehow got crossed."

"How do I know that name?" he asks, scratching his dark beard.

"He's a male stripper," Candy says. "He's also the bastard son of Jude Hallstead from that Hickory biker gang. Plus, he also knocked up Ruby Bauer, who thinks you're her Fairy Godmother. And you said I never do research."

Hayes smirks but doesn't look back at his wife. She's tapping her pen and daring him to turn around.

"What do you want?" he asks me.

"I'd like to discuss taking over Common Bend and running it for you."

"Take it over for the Brotherhood?"

"No, you'd own it like you own White Horse."

"What about your daddy?"

"He wants Common Bend. You'll have Common Bend. Daddy will *not* be pleased."

"Gotta love daddy issues," Candy says.

Hayes sizes me up. He's a giant man at around seven feet tall. Yet, if he's looking to intimidate me, he'll need to try harder.

"Follow me in the back, and we'll see what bullshit you're spewing."

When I walk past Candy, she applauds my success. Hayes's office smells like expensive cigars and a hint of pizza. I sit across from him and let the man frown for a full minute.

"Why the fuck would I want Common Fucking Bend?"

"You'd fucking want it because you've worked too fucking hard making White Fucking Horse a nice fucking place just for it to fall fucking apart over a shithole like Common Fucking Bend."

Hayes exhales hard, maybe realizing I'm mocking him. Or he sees this as a competition, and I just out-fucked him.

"Get to the point."

"Everyone knows the Brotherhood has wanted Common Bend for decades. The Reapers took it and kept it, but they had another president back then. Mojo and Howler think now is the time to take the town. They figure Cooper Johansson won't have the balls to go to war over a town outside of his Kentucky power source. They might be right, and that's bad for you."

Hayes shows no reaction. He also doesn't tell me to get the fuck out of his office, so I know he's intrigued.

"The Brotherhood should expand south toward Nashville. There's little point in going north since they'll hit a block of Reapers' territory. Common Bend is a waste of time, but it's an ego quest for the current president and VP. They'll take it, though. If you grabbed Common Bend first, you'd protect your investment here and build a line between the clubs. The less they interact, the less their crap will flood into White Horse."

"I still don't know how this benefits me. The initial expenditure makes any move risky."

"I doubt the Reapers want Common Bend, but they won't let it go to the Brotherhood. Right now, they barely control the town. We've already seen several coups and how their trouble taints White Horse. This is the town you care about. If you run Common Bend, that'll protect your investments here. If the Brotherhood runs Common Bend, though, they won't do much better than the Reapers because neither club cares about it. They'll both let the town fester, which isn't good for you."

"So, I take the town, and you run it. How would that work?"

"Take it might not be the right words. You'd buy Common Bend from the Reapers. I'd keep the drugs and other illegal businesses from coming to White Horse. You'd focus on your town, and I'd act as the manager for Common Bend."

"Would the Reapers sell it?"

"If you buy it, they can stick it to their rivals while ditching a problem."

"How much do you think I'd pay for the shithole?"

"Based on a cursory examination of their income from the town, they'd lose less than a million a year. Most of the meth is pissed away to the dealers, and the brothels pay too much for protection from the cops before the money ever reaches the club. I'd say less than ten million will be enough for them to write off the town. With proper management, you'd make that money back in around two years."

"And you'd be the proper management. Aren't you a fucking stripper?"

"I have no shame when it comes to making money. I don't mind shit assignments or taking crap from blowhard bosses. I'll just get the job done."

Hayes smirks at the blowhard thing. "This is about your daddy, right? You want to show him how you're the best bastard he ever jizzed."

"No, I want to take Common Bend from him. I'm not looking for a happy reunion. I want to make the old man suffer, and he wants Common Bend. That doesn't mean he'll treat the town any better than he does his jizz receptacles."

Leaning back in his giant chair, Hayes considers the logistics. He isn't tight with the Reapers, but he nurses a grudge against the Brotherhood. Mojo and Howler often piss trouble in the direction of White Horse.

Grudge or not, Hayes is a businessman first, and he isn't sure his investment is safe in the hands of a stranger.

"I was under the impression you were tight with the Rutgers twins," he finally says.

"I am."

"How do they feel about you shitting on the Brotherhood's plans?"

"They don't know, but they'll like it long term. Camden doesn't want to spend time and money on Common Bend. The twins want to go south. They'd also like a buffer between them and the Reapers. You'll give them what they want before they even take over."

"You know that for a fucking fact, or are you pulling theories out of your ass?"

"Somewhere in between."

Hayes crosses his massive arms and glares at me. "Did you tell anyone else about your brilliant fucking plan?"

"No."

"Well, you're working on a lot of maybes and guesses. You don't even know if the Reapers will sell Common Bend. I won't fight with them and the Brotherhood at the same time."

"Then send me to Kentucky to meet with Johansson and see if he's game. Once he gives you an answer, you can decide if my guesses and maybes are worth the investment."

"Send you, huh? On my dime, you mean?"

"Why the fuck not? You're not hurting for cash."

Hayes scratches at his beard again and then points at me. "If you leave town for a few days, don't you think someone might get a little curious about where you've gone? I don't want the Brotherhood getting their panties in a twist before I've decided anything."

Without thinking, I blurt out, "I'll take Ruby and our daughter, Chevelle, with me. No one is gonna think shit about us going away for a family weekend."

"Now, I'm paying for you and your family to take a vacation?"

Narrowing my gaze, I exhale slowly. "To a tiny town in Kentucky. Let's not pretend you're bankrolling a trip to Disney World over here."

Hayes gives me a weird frown before standing up. "Fine. Let me get some shit in order. I'll let Johansson know you're coming. You can work with Candy on the logistics of the trip. Hotel and that shit."

I consider complaining about how his wife doesn't take her job seriously. Rather than throwing shade at his woman, I only nod. We don't shake hands. Hayes doesn't even tell me goodbye.

I simply leave his office and explain to Candy how I'll call her later. Though she never looks up from her computer game, I sense she'll get all the details as soon as I'm out the door.

EIGHTEEN - RUBY

Sally and I decide to check out other Italian restaurants in the area to see what the competition serves. I invite Harmony and Keanu to join Elle and us since my sister is lonely without Daisy.

We drive to nearby White Horse to eat at Pizza & Meatballs. The restaurant is so new that the ladies' room still smells like paint. The service sucks, even if the food is decent.

"De Campo's made really good meatballs," Harmony says, helping Keanu with his cheese pizza.

Nodding, I did like their meatballs. "I think the Hallstead sisters want a classy menu, but that won't sell with a town full of rednecks who only want pizza and spaghetti."

"No, but I can already tell they don't want to decide anything," Sally says with a mouthful of lasagna. "That's why they hired us. We need to make the decisions. They're only involved to piss off the Brotherhood."

I wish my mother didn't mention the club's name in White Horse. The locals aren't friendly to the trash that blows in from nearby towns like Hickory Creek or Common Bend. At least, that's what White Horse's top thug likes to say.

As if beckoned by my thought of him, Angus Hayes enters the restaurant with his wife and her two kids in tow. They get the best table in a corner where the huge man can spread out. Even though he once helped me out of a jam in Common Bend, I avoid looking at him. Well, technically, he had two assassins help me out. But for him, it's the thought that counts.

Despite my efforts to ignore him, Hayes stares right at me. With his size and power, he never needs to be subtle. But damn, he isn't even pretending he doesn't want to dig into my brain from across the room.

Leaning forward, I whisper, "Can you guys do me a favor and all look at Hayes at the same time? Really stare at him like he's staring at me."

"Is that a good idea?" Harmony asks.

"Men need to know their place," Sally instantly says. "Where is he?"

Once I point at Hayes, we all stare straight in his direction. The asshole doesn't flinch because he's Angus Fucking Hayes and can have us killed. I do catch a hint of a grin before he leans toward his wife. Soon, she's eyeballing us, too. Then, her kids notice and stare in our direction.

The family-versus-family staring contest continues for nearly a minute. I'm ready to give up until several loud rednecks enter. Hayes loses interest in me and focuses his dark glare on the newcomers.

The big jerk acts like White Horse is his personal plaything, and no one can join in unless they get his permission first. Clearly, these rude people didn't get the message.

Relieved he's no longer focused on me, I return to eating. "I hope he doesn't think I owe him because he helped me out."

"Well, you do owe him," Harmony says.

Sally shakes her head. "She owes no one. He helped because he wanted to, not because he was doing Ruby a favor."

"Big words about a man who can make people disappear," Harmony says, challenging our mother.

"He doesn't waste time with people like us. A man like him has bigger bodies to bury."

"I still don't know why he's giving me the stink-eye," I mutter. "I saw him months ago while shopping at the mall. He didn't even give me a second glance."

"Maybe he's giving Mom the stink-eye," Harmony says, still challenging our mother.

Sally frowns at her youngest child. "No, he doesn't like tie-dye."

"Or people who talk too loud."

Elle glances back and forth between the shit-talking women, probably hoping she'll be old enough soon to join in.

"Or grown women wearing a barrette in her hair like a child," Sally mutters.

"Or people who still talk too loud."

Sally and Harmony laugh at their shit-talking, but I remain nervous. I've spent a good long time staying under the radar of bad men. Even in high school, I was wary of dating Bonn because his dad was the VP of a motorcycle club.

I craved safety in a town where too many girls courted trouble. People called me dull or a party-pooper, but I wanted to survive to my thirties in one piece. A goal I plan to keep.

NINETEEN - BONN

Chevelle bounces into the apartment and barrels into me. Her perfect little face stares up, and she gives me a smile missing two front teeth. Behind her, Ruby stands awkwardly. I ignore the grumpy mama while walking with Chevelle into the kitchen.

"I got second place in our race at school today."

I throw up my hand, and she slaps hers against it. "I knew you were fast."

"I don't have homework. Mom already helped me with it."

Ruby remains near the door, having shut it but refusing to embrace the apartment fully.

"Can you watch TV while I talk to your mom for a minute?"

When Chevelle looks at her mother, Ruby stares back. They share a silent conversation. I don't know what they say, but I think Chevelle wins. My girl skips to the couch and turns on the TV while Ruby inches closer.

"I have a load of laundry," she awkwardly says.

"Why are you acting weird?"

"How am I supposed to act?"

"I don't know."

Ruby looks at my lips, and then her gaze darts upward. Smiling, I take a step toward her and erase the pesky space between us.

"I've missed you," I whisper and lean down to kiss her.

Ruby pulls away before suddenly lifting her lips. She shows as much uncertainty when I kiss her. One moment, her body tenses. The next, she wraps her arms around my waist and melts against me.

I'm forced to end the kiss when my erection threatens to tear through my jeans, followed by her jeans until my dick finds its way inside her.

"You taste like sex," I mumble and mentally order my dick to kneel.

Ruby steps back and shakes her head. "I will never forgive you," she spits out, even though her eyes are begging me to kiss her again.

"Well, what I'm about to say won't make you like me more."

Her lust-filled eyes narrow, and I see anger awakening in them. "What?"

"Let me help you with your laundry."

Ruby gives me a side frown before walking away. I follow her to the laundry room, my gaze focused on her clingy pair of leggings.

"Stop looking at my butt," she mutters without glancing back at me.

"If only I could."

Shaking her head, Ruby likely smiles, but she refuses to let me see. She hides her face behind her hair as she dumps her dirty clothes into the washer and turns it on.

"So, what's the bad news?" she finally asks, crossing her arms and scowling at me.

"Not bad news. More like a business opportunity."

"If this is about your stripping job, I don't want to hear it."

"Nope, but thanks for reminding me of my crap job every chance you get."

"You're welcome," she mumbles, now struggling to keep her lips from curling into a smile.

"Hayes is willing to let me run Common Bend for him if I can convince the leader of the Reapers Motorcycle Club in Kentucky to sell the territory."

"No," Ruby says instantly.

"You haven't heard the details."

"You need to stop before this goes too far."

"Stop what?"

"Making deals with men who will murder you for failing. What are you even thinking?" she says, breathing too fast.

"Ruby, every night, I lie awake thinking about how I want to do right by Chevelle. By you too, but what can I accomplish with my skills? I'm not great at construction. I nearly flooded a house trying to install plumbing. There's no way I could get through college. While I could ask to work for the Brotherhood and play nice with my dad, I don't want to owe that jackass."

"No, you want to piss off the jackass by working for another jackass he hates."

"Hayes runs White Horse like a business. He gets things done and then goes home to his wife and kids. Why can't I have that? Why does everything have to be long nights of drinking and bar hoes? That's the Brotherhood's way, but Hayes acts like a businessman, and I could, too. I know Common Bend, and I can organize shit. I'm better at that than fixing roofs."

"You make it sound simple, but I know this is about wanting to screw over Howler."

"You're wrong. It's about you and Chevelle and me, too. Do you think I enjoy shaking my ass for screaming women? It's fucking gross having them touching me and shoving dollar bills in my pants. I do it because I need to make enough money to do right by Chevelle. Construction can't get me a decent place to live or money in the bank for her college. If I can make this work with Hayes and Common Bend, I can offer her security. I'll do it with my clothes on."

Ruby runs her hands through her hair, pulling at it in frustration. "If you're looking for my approval, that ain't happening. Your big idea could leave Elle fatherless, and she'd be destroyed without you."

"If this works out, can you imagine us living in Common Bend?"

"Us?" she balks as if the thought of us together had never crossed her mind.

"New two-unit townhomes are coming up in Common Bend. I thought if you and I couldn't work together, we could still be friends and live next to each other."

"That is never going to happen."

"Can you imagine Chevelle walking back and forth between her two homes?"

Shaking her head, Ruby doesn't want to hear my ideas. Yet, I notice interest lingering in her eyes.

"The neighborhood I'm talking about is close to White Horse, where the schools are better. In fact, we might have enough money to send Chevelle to a Catholic school. She'd get a better education than here in Hickory."

"I like living close to my mom and Harmony," Ruby defiantly states, her jaw rigid now.

"The trailer park is changing. The old-timers are dying off, and the new people moving in are rougher. It's not how things were when we were kids."

"I don't want to live next to you."

"Down the road or wherever you want. If this job works out, I'll be able to help you find a good place. You wouldn't have to worry about money. You could find a job you like better than waitressing."

"I don't mind my job."

Resting my hands on my hips, I frown. "You'll disagree with everything because I'm saying it."

"I can't agree to anything involving Angus Hayes."

"Didn't he help you out a few years back when the Common Bend sheriff was after you?"

Ruby's frown is momentarily replaced by her surprise. "How did you know about that?"

"The twins knew, and they have big mouths."

"Yes, he helped me, but only because it benefited him. Hayes is a shrewd man and will cut you loose if you aren't living up to his standards. And by 'cut you loose,' I mean dump your body somewhere."

"That's not going to happen."

"Why not?"

"Because I'm not reckless, and I'll never promise him anything I can't deliver."

"This won't end well."

"Or it'll end with us having everything we need."

"Life doesn't work like that."

"Don't get started on life. I mean, how many people said we were too young to be good parents? Well, fuck them because we've done a great job with Chevelle. She always

71

feels loved, and that's because we put in the work to make sure she feels that way. When we focus and work hard, we can take from life whatever we want."

"And if you're wrong?"

I take her hands in mine. To my surprise, she lets me hold them.

"This is my chance to do something big, and I don't think I'll get another one. I'm not a kid anymore, and I see no other way to make a move in life. This is it, and I'll always regret not trying."

When Ruby stares into my eyes, I'm taken aback by the fear in her gaze.

"What if your big chance ends you?"

"Then, help me make it work."

"How?"

"I need to go to Kentucky to meet with the Reapers' leader. If I leave town, it'll look weird since I never go anywhere. If you and Chevelle come with me, the Brotherhood won't think a damn thing about us taking a trip."

"You want to take our daughter to meet these people?"

"They won't hurt her. Or me. These aren't low-level junkie losers we're talking about. They run their club like a business, and I'm coming to them with Hayes's backing."

"No."

"It's a small town in Kentucky. You and Chevelle can stay at a hotel. I found one with an indoor pool. Think of it as a little vacation while I work."

"No."

"Please, Ruby, help me with this," I nearly beg.

"No."

"That refusal sounded a little less certain," I say, nudging her with my knee. "You could take off a few days from work and hang out with Chevelle. How much would she love swimming?"

Ruby closes her eyes, fighting against her urge to tell me no again. She's right to be nervous. I'm worried, too. We both know I won't be able to afford this apartment in a few years when I'm nearing thirty, and the sheen has worn off my good looks.

Opening her eyes, Ruby crosses her arms and stares hard at me. "Promise if things go south that you'll bail on the entire thing."

"I'm doing this to improve things for us, not to make them worse. I'll bail before I let anything happen to you or Chevelle."

Ruby's gaze softens, and she nods. "I'm fucking stupid to agree, but I know the Brotherhood's been tense lately."

"Tense about what?"

"I don't know. Whenever the members come into the restaurant, they're on edge. I avoid working their tables because they make me nervous."

"Well, they'll be pissed if Hayes takes over Common Bend."

"You'll put a target on your back," she says, her voice cracking.

"They won't kill me. You know that, and I know that. The twins will eventually run the club, and they'll never sign off on my death. I can't see Mojo agreeing, either. My father wouldn't give two shits, but his sisters would. They like to pretend family means something around here."

"You better be right," Ruby says, poking my chest, "because you're about to piss off very dangerous men."

"And align with other dangerous men. I know it sounds crazy," I say, taking her poking hand and caressing the palm with my thumb. "But the payoff for us is worth it."

"There's no us, Bonn."

"Even if you never let me back into your heart, there'll always be an us."

Ruby says nothing, yet the emotion in her gaze betrays her silence. My plan terrifies her. My love scares her even more. But she agrees to the first and longs for the second. Now, I need to put everything together and prove her fears are worth the prize.

TWENTY - RUBY

Few things piss me off more than keeping secrets from my family. We share everything, always knowing our information is safe. Now, with Daisy married to Camden and Bonn ready to screw over the Brotherhood, I'm forced to hide something big from my sister. Worse still, I need to decide whether I can even share with Harmony without forcing her to lie to Daisy.

Since visiting Bonn, I've quietly packed two small bags for the trip. Next, I've made it my mission to clean up the trailer. My theory is the hotel will be clean and organized, and returning to a messy home will depress the crap out of me. Finished inside, I sweep around my porch because nothing says obsessive behavior like organizing a gravel driveway.

"What's wrong?" asks my youngest sister as soon as she arrives home from work.

"Nothing," I lie, still sweeping like a madwoman.

"Did Bonn do something? Do you need ice cream?" she asks and then whispers, "Or a mojito?"

"No, I'm fine."

Harmony leaves me long enough to walk over to pick up Keanu from Charlie's trailer. Returning with her son, she keeps her gaze on me. I know she'll change her clothes and make Keanu a snack. She'll get things in order, and then she'll pounce on me until I give up my secrets. Harmony plays the laidback hippy chick, but she's relentless when she wants something.

I hide in the trailer when I know she's done with her evening routine. Elle watches me intently. She saw the suitcases but doesn't dare ask a question when she isn't ready for the answer. Even at eight, my baby knows when to hold back and examine a situation. I've taught her well. However, Harmony is having none of my silent bullshit.

"Elle, go hang with Nana Sally. She's playing with Keanu by the pond."

My daughter immediately agrees, having caught onto how Harmony will dig up whatever I'm hiding. Once she leaves the trailer, I walk into the kitchen, where my pint of ice cream beckons me.

"We can make this hard, or we can make this easy," Harmony says, blocking my exit. "What's it going to be, Ruby Whiskey Bauer?"

"If you want to know, you'll have to pry it out of me. I remain silent for your benefit."

Stepping closer, Harmony stretches. I don't know what her plan is, but it might involve wrestling. *She's really loosening up her muscles.*

"You're going to tell me, or I'm going to tell Mom a delicious lie. She'll tell Betty and Charlie the delicious lie. They'll tell others the delicious lie. Soon, the delicious lie will become an undeniable fact."

"What's the lie?"

"I haven't decided, but I suspect it'll involve you and Bonn and public sex."

"Don't even say such a thing," I growl, even though my hormones very much approve of sex of any kind with Bonn.

"I imagine a scenario where you two fuck as the car goes through the wash. In the end, the towel guys applaud. Of course, you're worried because pictures were taken."

"You are not a good sister."

Harmony gives me an evil smile. "If you don't share your secret with me, I'll claim he did you in the butt to ensure you didn't get pregnant. Now, fess up."

"Bad Harmony," I admonish, but she only stretches.

"Why are you moving around like that if you're planning to tell lies?"

"I pulled a few muscles today at work. Not everything is about you, Ruby."

"Fine," I say, giving in to my need for sugar. I take out the pint of coconut pineapple ice cream and find two spoons. "But if I tell you, then you can't tell anyone else. Do you really want to keep a secret from Mom and Daisy?"

"I keep lots of secrets from you guys."

"Like what?"

"Wouldn't be much of a secret if I told you. Especially now that I know how easily you give up yours."

"Fine," I mutter, digging into the ice cream. "Bonn made a deal with Angus Hayes to take over Common Bend. He needs to go to Kentucky to meet with some bikers. Bonn asked me to come with him, so the twins and the Brotherhood won't think anything is up. I agreed, but now I'm having second thoughts. I'll still probably go since Bonn painted a vivid picture of what life could be like if this deal goes through. For one thing, he'd no longer strip. You know how I hate chicks looking at him nearly naked. But this deal will make him an enemy of the Brotherhood, so I can't tell Daisy anything because she'll tell Camden. Or she won't tell him, and I'll be responsible for her keeping secrets from her husband."

Harmony dips her spoon into the ice cream and takes a bite. "Why would Bonn want to work with Hayes instead of with the Brotherhood?"

"Because Howler is an asshole."

"But Howler and Mojo won't be in charge for much longer."

"Who told you that?"

"Everyone knows that."

"Was it Dayton?"

"No. He says his dad will never retire, and Camden will die an old man waiting for his chance."

"Well, there you go."

"Do you think Camden will wait? He has the backing of the Hallsteads, and I think the club gets backing from people in Memphis. I doubt a bunch of goons in Elvistown will want Mojo and Howler hanging on forever."

"You know a lot."

Harmony shrugs. "Dayton got drunk and told me stuff. He was probably bullshitting about half of it, but I think some of it must have been true."

"Why can't it all be true?"

"Dayton always lies. He says he can't trust himself to tell the truth."

"He's an idiot."

76

"No, not really, but he's lazy, and acting like an idiot keeps people from expecting too much. Now, let's get back to Bonn. So, if he works with Hayes, he'll do what in Common Bend?"

"Run it for Hayes."

"How does that make him the Brotherhood's enemy?"

"They want Common Bend."

"Why?"

"Didn't Dayton tell you that?"

"That might have been part of what I thought he was lying about. I don't know. He talked a lot that night, and he was drunk, so I had trouble following it all. I just wanted to make out, but he was a frigging chatterbug."

"I'm sure his father would love knowing that."

"Mojo only cares about Camden, who was too stupid to act stupid. Now, everyone expects him to be smart."

"Wise words."

"Not really."

"I feel like either Bonn is making a huge mistake, or he'll succeed like a fucking boss. I'm leaning toward the first one."

"If he fails, it's not so bad. The Brotherhood won't mess with him in a real way. The twins are close to him, and the Hallstead sisters won't like anything happening to Bonn. They might not care the way we do, but they still protect their family."

"I don't know," I say, jamming a big bite of ice cream into my mouth and immediately suffering a brain freeze.

Harmony smiles at my expression. "A weekend away will be fun."

"I saw something hopeful in Bonn's eyes when he was telling me his plan, and I got excited in a way I haven't felt in so long. I could get on board with the idea of not living paycheck to paycheck and having some savings. Living somewhere nicer, too. It sometimes bothers me how Elle goes to his nice condo and then comes back to this dump."

"The trailer isn't a dump. Mine is quite nice."

"Damn, hippy."

Harmony grins. "Let me ask you something, and you need to be square with me. No bullshit, safe answer. Be super honest with yourself. Is the real reason you're freaking about this trip because you know you and Bonn will bone?"

"Not in the least."

"How long will you be gone?"

"A few days."

"Are you staying in a hotel?"

"Yes."

Harmony walks to my fridge and digs around for a soda. "You'll see how great he is with Elle. That'll make you imagine what you can have as a family. Once your guard is down, your libido will take over. Bonn is a handsome man, and he wants you. The next thing you know, it'll be boning time."

"I think you're the one looking to get boned."

"Probably. So, does this hotel have a pool?"

"Yes."

"Bonn will be shirtless and wet."

Sighing, I scoop another spoonful of ice cream. "We're totally going to bone."

"Good because until you get sex off your brain, you won't be able to look at Bonn clearly."

"I'm not that horny."

"Yes, you are, but that's not why it's bound to happen. Bonn's previous sexual experience was with Kim Crawley. A primal part of you needs to reclaim him. Ever since you found out about them, you've had an urge to take back what she stole. That's one reason you think of her whenever you see him. She left her mark, and you need to erase it before you can see the real Bonn."

"That's very profound, but I think you're full of shit."

"Nope. I remember when you were crying and saying how he was yours. 'She fucked what was mine' is exactly how you put it once. Now is the time to reclaim him. That's all I'm saying. Boning doesn't mean you'll stay together, but it'll get Kim out of the equation."

"I don't want to agree with you."

"I know."

"But you're probably right."

"I know that, too," Harmony says, stretching out on the couch.

"I guess there's no denying we'll bone on the trip."

"Do you know what that means?"

"That I can't hide from my feelings anymore?"

"No, you'll need to shave," Harmony says with a look of horror. "Like all over. You're a hairy chick, and this is the big show. You'll need to prepare."

"You've been a pain in my ass since the day you were born."

"I think you're confusing me with Daisy," Harmony says, giggling to herself.

"Probably. So, will you watch Elle tonight while I dig out the hedge clippers?"

"I bet Billy would let you use his weed wacker to trim back your overgrown hedges."

"You're the worst, but I might run to the store for Nair. No waxing, though. A cheating man doesn't deserve a waxed beaver."

"And I didn't deserve that visual."

"Didn't you?" I ask, coming after her.

"No," she says, jumping up and racing out the trailer. "I've never been anything but helpful."

"Didn't you mention something about a weed wacker?"

Harmony scurries toward the pond where she plans to use Mom for cover. Keanu sees her first and goes running in her direction. The two collide and tumble into a giggling ball on the ground.

I can't be nearly as jovial with beaver prep in my near future. When I tell Mom about my trip with Bonn, she smiles and says she's happy for me. Sally knows I'm holding back, but I distract her with whispers of sex and beaver care. Waving me off, she assures me she can watch Elle overnight if it takes me that long to tame my hairy monster.

These are the moments when I'm smacked in the face with the downside of being so close to my family. No doubt, the entire trailer park will hear of my trimming duties by the end of the day.

79

In fact, two hours later, Daisy texts to warn me of going overboard and ending up bald. As punishment for her help, I send her a nudie beaver picture I snag off the internet. An hour later, Harmony says Dayton texted her to say he saw the picture and thinks my coin purse looks cold.

Never has leaving town felt so perfectly timed.

TWENTY ONE - BONN

The condo won't be my home once I make a deal with Hayes. In fact, all of Hickory Creek Township might prove to be off-limits. I've already started looking at housing in Common Bend. I even drove by a few places and imagined Chevelle playing with the kids I saw.

Earlier this morning, Hayes texted to say the trip is on, and I need to get my shit in order. The Reapers and Cooper Johansson will see me next weekend. Not before. Not after. I have one shot at selling the deal.

Downstairs, the condo houses a small gym I use daily. I'm less worried about staying in shape for my job as I am about working off my pent-up sexual energy. Nearly nine years without sex will make a man fucking crazy. Kissing Ruby only intensified the need, so I add an extra hour to my workout routine to ensure I won't sport a hard-on all day.

A few minutes after I start running on the treadmill, Dayton stumbles into the gym, wearing only tattered sweat shorts. He looks at me, rubs his sleepy eyes, and shuffles closer.

"You should wear shoes in here," I tell Dayton.

"Why?"

"I'm sure you have a few foot diseases."

Dayton glances down at his feet before grinning at me. "Banging whores doesn't lead to diseases on your feet. If you got laid in the last decade, you'd know that."

"That isn't where I thought you picked up your foot diseases. I mean, man, you walk fucking barefoot in parking lots."

"Sometimes, I can't find my shoes, and I've got to roll."

When I say nothing, Dayton stops pretending to exercise on the treadmill and sits on the floor in front of me. I watch him yawn again before he rolls onto his back and rests sprawled on the floor.

"I didn't come in here to exercise," he mumbles while hiding his face under an arm to block the sunlight.

"Why are you here, then?"

"To talk to you."

Running steadily, I remain steely-eyed even if my gut leaps in fear. Did Hayes rat me out? Were the twins keeping tabs on me and know about the deal I made? I'm not ready for my plan to fall apart before I even get started.

"What about?" I ask.

"About Ruby and her mom."

His answer messes with my balance, and I nearly fly off the treadmill. Regaining my senses, I keep running and avoid an injury.

"What about them?"

"Did you know my mom and her sisters bought De Campo's pizza place?"

"No."

"Well, they did, and they also met with Ruby and Sally. I wanted to know what the meeting was about."

"Why are you asking me?"

"Aren't you dating your old lady?"

"We didn't talk about De Campo's."

"She must have said something about meeting with my mom."

"Nope."

Dayton removes his arm from his face and frowns up at me. "Dude, I don't believe you."

"Dude, you don't need to believe me."

"What if I threatened you? Would you tell me, then?"

"No."

"This is serious shit."

"You'd sound more convincing if you weren't hungover."

"I could have Camden threaten you. Now that Daisy cuckolds him, he never drinks. You gotta pity the ball-less fucker."

"I don't know anything about De Campo's or the Hallsteads. Ruby and I are focused on us, not whatever your family is doing."

Dayton stands up and steadies himself by holding onto my treadmill. He eyes the controls before hitting the button to make me run faster.

"The Brotherhood wanted De Campo's place."

"Okay."

"We had plans for it. When De Campo didn't want to sell, someone burned it down. Do you get my drift?"

"Yes, but I don't know why I should care."

"You should care because my mom is starting shit with the Brotherhood, and she's wrangled your old lady into the deal."

"Ruby is a smart woman. She'll make the right decision."

"Decision about what?" he asks, hitting the button again and speeding up my treadmill.

"About whatever your mom wants from her."

"Why don't you call her right now and find out what they talked about?"

"Why don't you fuck off and find out yourself?" I ask, stopping the treadmill and stepping off. "Clara is your damn mother. If you want to know what they talked about, go fucking ask her."

"If only it were so simple."

Smiling, I wipe sweat from my neck and face. "You're scared of your mom, so you want me to do your dirty work. What a pussy."

Dayton grins. "My mom can be fucking scary. You don't even know."

"Look, I get how your parents are having a pissing match, but that's not my problem. It's not yours, either. If you were smart, you'd stay out of the crossfire. That way, whoever loses won't blame you."

Dayton runs a hand through his messy, shoulder-length blond hair. He looks ready for a long nap. A few weeks in rehab wouldn't hurt, either.

"Camden doesn't like Howler's favored bastard son. That keeps him on the outside since Howler has my father's ear. I'm the only one thinking smart and playing along with the new guy's shit."

"So, when you act like an asshole, that's you undercover?"

Dayton narrows his eyes. "I don't like being mocked."

"No one does, buddy. It's a pretty universal dislike."

"Look, I'm smart while Camden is in love. He can't see past Daisy's pussy long enough to think of our future."

"Howler's kid won't take the club. You're the president's sons. You and Camden were groomed for the top two spots. This guy, JJ, hasn't proven he's anything more than a kiss-ass."

"How would you know?"

"Your brother talks and he sees plenty despite Daisy's pussy distracting him. You should be having this conversation with Camden instead of me. I don't know anything about the Hallsteads, the Brotherhood, or De Campo's. I'm just trying to get back together with Ruby. Nothing more complicated than that."

Dayton struggles against another yawn. He glances around the gym and then yanks up his shorts.

"I'll take your advice for what it's worth."

"Whatever. Now, can I return to working out without you stalking me?"

"I'm not stalking you."

"Feels like it when you stare at me while I'm half-naked. Something unpleasant about the entire thing."

Dayton isn't sure if I'm messing with him. He watches me for a long damn time before shrugging and walking to the door.

"Good luck with your old lady."

I wait until Dayton's out of sight before I exhale my fear. While I don't doubt my cousins would refuse to off me if the Brotherhood wanted me gone, I also know JJ has proven himself more than willing to deal with club problems. De Campo's was the first shot across the bow and the likely reason Clara and the other Hallstead sisters are firing back. I hope my move with Hayes doesn't start a full-fledged war.

84

TWENTY TWO - RUBY

Elle bounces around the trailer park lot while Bonn and I pack the SUV. Though I've certainly packed too many things, I'm paranoid I'll forget something crucial. To be safe, I bring half of my trailer along with two small suitcases.

"They'll have pillows," Bonn says when I shove a few into the back seat next to Elle, who now bounces inside the car.

"I don't know what kind, and I'm picky."

"Okay."

"Don't patronize me."

"Don't snap at me just because you're tense."

I want to slug him, mostly because he's right. Sighing, I stare at the overstuffed SUV.

"Should I take a bunch of stuff back?"

Bonn flinches when he sees me tearing up. Cupping my cheek, he kisses my forehead with his warm lips. "Don't get upset. You can snap at me if you want."

"Really?"

"Yes, but just until you stop crying."

"It's not even that," I mumble, wiping my eyes. "This trip is a big deal, and I'm scared, and I want to bail, but I can't because Elle is so excited, and I'd be the horrible bitch who ruined her fun."

"Yes, she would hate you if you bailed."

When I glare at him, Bonn only smiles and shuts the back of the SUV. "Let's get going before you decide we need to bring an actual kitchen sink."

Giving in to my urge to smile, I fake-punch him in the arm. "You better be on your best behavior with me."

"Same goes for you."

Despite his casual grin, his words hold a hint of a threat. I figure I better let it drop and avoid starting a fight before we even get on the road. Except not knowing will drive me nuts the entire trip.

Before Bonn can walk away, I grab him by the arm. "What does that mean? Are you threatening me?"

"Yes, and you better learn to watch yourself. Do we understand each other?"

Stepping back, I don't know how to react. Normally, I'd harden up and protect Elle and maybe hurt the threat. With Bonn, I can only stare shocked at his steely gaze.

"Oh, Ruby, this is going to be a long trip," he says, suddenly laughing. "You should see your face right now."

"It's not funny."

"Yes, it really is. You're terrified of me, and I've never once been in charge in this relationship. Did I even get to pick a single place we ate at during the entire time we dated?"

"You picked that shithole we went to the other day."

Bonn wraps a lock of my hair around his index finger. "Yes, because you stubbornly refused to choose. I only got to wear the pants because you threw them at me."

"Whatever."

Bonn smiles wider and taps my nose with his index finger. "You do need to understand something about me, though."

"What's that?" I ask, wanting to be angry at his teasing but just relieved my Bonn wasn't replaced with a raging jackass.

"You are the only woman I want. I will wait for you for however long it takes, but I will never give up. Not next year or in ten or when we're old people living in a retirement home. If you find another man, I will follow you around on dates and ruin things. That way, you'll be forced to be alone or with me."

Bonn's dark eyes shine with a hint of malice, and I can't look away.

"I'll be unrelenting but in a passive way. That's who I am. I don't shove you down and take what I want, but I'll wait. It's been eight years without you. My poor penis shriveled up a few times and once climbed inside me in protest because I refused to give it to another woman. My head and heart are running the show, though, and they

86

demand you. So, you can play cold on our trip, and I will wait. You can keep me at arm's length for as long as you need, but this is happening eventually. Even if you only give in out of fatigue, I'll take it."

"That's pathetic."

"Maybe for a guy like Camden whose ego must dominate everyone around him. Pathetic or not, I know what I want, and I won't settle for anything less. I also know what you need, and I won't let you settle for anyone else."

"Stop threatening my future, possible boyfriends."

"They can't make you happy."

"Yeah, because you're stalking us."

Bonn grins at the thought of scaring those hypothetical men. "No, because they're not me. If they were better than me, they would romance you until you were blind to everything else. No, your future, possible boyfriends are failures before they even show up. You might as well preemptively ditch them."

"Despite your threats, I'm wearing my most unflattering pajamas on this trip. That way, you'll remember I don't want to be seduced."

"Flannel? Really? You know for a fact that shit makes my dick raging hard. You damn minx."

Bonn laughs at my irritation before walking to the driver's door. He gives the area one last look before getting inside. Sliding into the passenger seat, I inhale Bonn's scent. His used SUV is pristine, much like his condo. We're both rather anal about cleanliness. I glance quickly in his direction and find him studying me. His dark gaze is too intense in the enclosed space. I hate how I can't catch my breath when he does nothing more than watch me.

"Elle," I say as if she's my lifeline to sex-free sanity.

Turning toward the back seat, Bonn and I find Elle watching the tablet he bought for her birthday.

"Yeah, Mom?" she asks, beaming at me.

"Are you ready to go?"

Elle glances at her father before nodding. I see so much of Bonn in her beautiful face. Rather than play the role of my lifeline, Elle is one more reminder of what I gain if I dare lower my guard with Bonn.

.

TWENTY THREE – BONN

Trees are a crap distraction from the thought of sharing a room with Ruby tonight. When I explained Hayes was paying for the trip, she decided to book a single room. That way, I'll owe him less. So, she'll share a bed with Elle while I'll be a good boy by staying in the other. If she thinks separate beds will keep us from finding our way together, Ruby has lost her damn mind.

"I heard you and Sally are working on a project for the Hallstead sisters," I say when Ruby remains silent.

"We're helping them put together a restaurant where De Campo's used to be. We'll manage the place after it opens. At least, that's what they say, but who knows with the Hallstead family."

"Are you still waitressing?"

"Yes, part-time. I plan to quit when the new restaurant is closer to opening."

"How did this all come together?"

"Clara called Sally, and I went to the meeting with her. It seemed like a chance at a better schedule and more money, so I said yes. Sally is still working full-time. She doesn't trust they won't ditch the restaurant once they've properly pissed off the Brotherhood."

I don't mention how Sally is right to be worried. Ruby no doubt knows the Hallsteads have only one interest in mind, and that's the Hallsteads.

"It's great that you're trying something new."

"Big shock that you'd think that."

Smiling, I take her hand and keep it in mine on the armrest. Ruby watches me, considers yanking her hand free, and decides to let herself enjoy my affection. The small gesture is a big fucking win for me.

Soon, Chevelle asks to stop at McDonald's for lunch. She dances out of the car and into the restaurant. I don't doubt she dances in the bathroom with her mom, too. While we eat, she tells me she feels like a princess. Ruby flinches at

Chevelle's declaration. I know she fears our second chance will be a flop. If we fail this time around, our hearts aren't the only ones on the line.

When I smile reassuringly at Ruby, she takes my gesture wrong. Or possibly, she needs to be mad again. Either way, she doesn't return my smile or talk to me for the rest of lunch. She's in such a rotten mood that she joins Chevelle in the back seat for the rest of the drive.

Now, I'm in a bad mood. I watch her in the rearview and wonder why she can't mellow out for a single day. I know she wants to, but her pride refuses to let her forgive me. Not even long enough for her to enjoy something she craves.

I turn on the radio to distract from how the SUV now reeks of hostility and hurt feelings. Chevelle turns off her tablet and sings along with the music. Even though the songs are from the 1980s, my girl knows the words. *Ruby and I raised her well.*

Chevelle gets loud and dramatic while singing, "In a Big Country." Her performance finally mellows Ruby's crappy mood. They sway together, singing and clapping their hands. By the end of the song, I've lost my frown and feel a little more hopeful about the rest of the trip.

We arrive at the Holiday Inn Express at the first Ellsberg exit. After checking in, I drag a cart full of Ruby's crap to the room. She wants to frown at me. Yet, every time a pillow falls off the mountain of luggage, she rolls her eyes and grins at how much she overpacked.

Chevelle rushes into the room, touching everything from the shiny countertops to the stark white blankets on the two queen-sized beds. She momentarily stares out of the window before running over to the big screen TV.

"Which one is ours, Mom?" Chevelle asks, butt-bouncing on the first bed now.

"I'm always hot, so let's pick the one by the air conditioner," Ruby says, organizing the suitcases. "Is that all right?"

"I'm fine either way."

"I think we can take some of this back to the SUV and leave it there," Ruby says, waiting for me to tease her for overpacking.

"I'm tired. We'll do it later."

Realizing I have no interest in giving her trouble, she walks to where Chevelle plays with the remote.

"Can we go swimming today?" Chevelle asks, ditching her bed to sit with me on mine.

"Sure."

Jumping off the bed, she digs out her swimsuit and gets dressed. I glance at Ruby watching me.

"Do you want me to take her?" I ask.

"Are you kidding? I want to swim, too."

"Can I come?"

"Don't be a baby, Bonn," she says, sliding off the bed. "You don't have to beg or whine. Just come or don't."

I smile at her tone, which makes her frown darken, which only makes me smile wider.

"Stop," she growls.

"I haven't seen you in a swimsuit in a long time. I might rip through my swim trunks."

Ruby's eyes widen. "She's in the next room."

"She's singing and not paying attention to us."

"You should still be careful."

"Okay, Mom," I mumble while looking for my swim trunks.

"Now, you're trying to irritate me."

"Why not? You've been in a bad mood for hours. Why pretend otherwise?"

"Then, why are you smiling?"

"I told you," I say, finding my trunks. "I get to see you half-naked today. That's worth whatever attitude you throw my way."

Ruby shakes her head. "I wouldn't get your hopes up."

"What does that mean?"

"I have a mom body now. No way you're ripping through anything."

"Okay," I mumble, fighting the urge to laugh.

"Stop it."

91

"I'm ready to rip out of my jeans right now, and you're fully dressed."

"I've let myself go," she says with complete seriousness.

"I can tell. It's a sexy look on you."

"I'm going to smother you in your sleep," she hisses, baring her teeth.

"But not until after I see you half-naked. Seems worth it to me."

Ruby gives up trying to be angry and smiles slightly. "This is a nice hotel. Thank you for bringing us."

Walking to where she stands with her swimsuit hanging limply from her hand, I caress her soft cheek.

"You're everything," I say, causing her to flinch. Before Ruby can respond, I walk to the bathroom where Chevelle sings in the mirror. "I hate to interrupt your performance, but I need to get naked, and your mom won't let me do it in the bedroom."

Chevelle laughs at me and then runs into the room to laugh at her mom. She's so hyper now that I think she'd laugh at pretty much anything. Hopefully, an hour in the pool will wear her out some. Otherwise, I can't imagine her sleeping tonight. Especially not early enough to allow Ruby and me a little time alone.

TWENTY FOUR - RUBY

I've rarely been an insecure woman. When Daisy worried about fitting in, I was more concerned with people leaving me the hell alone. I always stood out anyway as one of the few non-lily-white girls in a pond overflowing with lilies.

With Bonn, I never suffered a shy moment. We were each other's first, and the sex was great because we were us. Even if he was the most beautiful boy in our school, he never felt out of reach to me. Bonn was mine. I knew him, and he knew me. That's why I was never shy about running around naked together.

Now, I'm nervous in a one-piece swimsuit. I wish I had a beach towel to wrap myself in, so I could hide how age has given my butt a little too much meat. I normally enjoy the extra padding, especially when sitting on the ground. Today, though, I feel like a lumpy mess.

My confidence certainly isn't helped by Bonn's chiseled physique. He doesn't have an ounce of fat or flaw on his entire body. I already knew he looked perfect, but him strutting in only a pair of swim trunks leaves nothing to the imagination. He's a hard, sleek warrior while I'm a human woman with human woman flaws like a jiggly butt and cellulite on my hips.

So obsessed with comparing our bodies, I barely hear Elle telling me how much she loves swimming and how she loves me and she loves her dad. She pretty much loves everyone in the world right now.

The pool area is empty when we arrive, so Bonn plays music on his phone. A catchy Depeche Mode song soothes my nerves long enough for me to get into the semi-warm water. Elle bounces nearby with Bonn.

"Can I get my hair wet?" she asks me twice before her words finally register.

"Yes. I brought a lot of conditioners."

Elle smiles at her dad and then dunks herself into the water. Coming back up, she laughs and wipes her eyes.

"Did you see?" she asks me when I stare at them.

"Yes, baby."

"Ignore her," Bonn tells Elle. "Let's race back and forth."

"It's too deep," I say with too much force.

Bonn frowns. "I meant on the shallow side."

"You're too tall," I mumble.

Bonn wades over to me and leans down. "I know you're having trouble focusing when I'm half-naked like this, but you need to settle down before I'm forced to tranq you."

Narrowing my eyes until they're tiny slits, I'm startled when he laughs.

"It's not funny."

"Soon, I'll enjoy what's under this suit," he says, running a finger along my belly. "You and I know that's coming, so you best just accept it and enjoy our trip."

Rolling my eyes, I hate his confidence. *Fucking Bonn and his fucking perfect abs.* When he turns away, I take in the sight of his muscular bronze back.

I wish I could relax like I normally do with Elle. Unfortunately, I feel less like a mother and more like a sex-starved harlot ready to jump the wet, half-naked man nearby. *Was my desire such a bad thing, though?*

My mother didn't give up her sex life when she had kids. She still craved male companionship. Romance may be a dead-end for her these days, but I had no doubt she hooked up regularly just to blow off some steam.

I hadn't done the same after Bonn because no one could compare to him. Now, he's at my disposal. If I made a move, he'd never say no. We could blow off some steam, and I could think straight.

Lust wasn't a weakness. Acting on that lust in a stupid way like Bonn did with Kim was what made him pathetic. Wanting someone was natural. *I'm a fucking woman, dammit!* I have needs, and Bonn is a gorgeous man. My throbbing clit and achy nipples aren't signs I've lost my mind, but that I haven't lost my libido from a lack of use.

Watching Bonn and Elle swim back and forth in the shallow end, I admire his body and remember what it was like to be with him. I lean against the wall and recall the way his hands felt on my body. How exciting it was to be so completely exposed to another person. The way our bodies became one in a magical yet animalistic way.

Sex had felt so amazing that it was all I thought about some days. My teenage hormones left me a slave to his touch. Tonight, I'll give my body a taste of what it once took for granted.

TWENTY FIVE - BONN

Ruby keeps fiddling with Chevelle's hair while we sit at Bojangles for dinner. Our girl's curls turn into a frizzy mess if not properly conditioned. Back when Ruby refused to speak to me, Sally had to dumb down the hair care process. In her still thick Brazilian accent, she told me not to fuck up the child's hair, or she'd return with Betty and Charlie. Though I wasn't particularly scared of three middle-aged women, I still made sure to do right by my daughter.

"What are you thinking about?" Chevelle asks with a mouth full of mashed potatoes.

"I'm happy to be here with you and your mom."

Chevelle smiles before immediately checking for her mother's reaction. Ruby shares our grin and even gives me an appreciative nod.

"Did you know your mom made the cheerleading team?" I ask Chevelle.

Like magic, Ruby's smile instantly disappears.

"You were a cheerleader?" Chevelle asks Ruby.

"No."

"She only went out for the team to prove she could make it. Your mom is stubborn that way."

Chevelle beams at Ruby. "Was it hard?"

"A little but boring, too. The other girls weren't very nice to each other."

"Were they mean to you?"

"No, because they thought I'd beat them up."

Laughing, Chevelle can't believe anyone would fear Ruby. Our daughter doesn't know the ugly details of her mother's life. Ruby is a big believer in lying to children. She once told me how she wished Sally lied about her father, so she might think better of him while growing up. Knowing the truth about the asshole dumped too much reality on her childhood. Blissfully unaware is the best kind of bliss, she explained.

"Did you know your mom was a teacher's pet in social studies class in high school?"

"You were?"

Ruby shrugs casually, but she's shooting me pissed daggers.

"She was a bit of a nerd," I tell Chevelle, who giggles at her mom. "She liked reading about other places."

"Like Aunt Daisy."

"Yes, but I don't want to learn a bunch of languages like her. I'm happy with Portuguese and just enough Spanish to get by."

"Dad was your boyfriend in school," Chevelle says, giggling again and likely remembering information her aunts shared.

Still glaring at me, Ruby nods. "He was the prettiest boy in the entire school."

Chevelle looks at me and starts laughing. I don't know what's so funny, but she doesn't stop until she's snorted a few times and gotten the hiccups.

"Look at what you did," Ruby mutters to me.

"You made her laugh," I say, smiling. "You always were funny."

Ruby desperately wants me to shut up. I see it in her angry eyes and twitching jaw and, of course, in her clenching fists. Despite her signals, I can't stop.

"Your mom made blue eye shadow popular at our school, and that hadn't been cool in like twenty years."

Chevelle runs a finger over Ruby's eyelid while her mother frowns at me.

"You were the prettiest girl in school," I murmur, and her scowl falters. "You looked like a movie star slumming it in a teen flick. I couldn't believe you were real."

Ruby shakes her head, unhappy with the praise. Or maybe she can feel how much I crave her. Chevelle only hears the compliments and knows her mom was cool. While all kids want to believe their parents are special, Chevelle isn't oblivious to how different she looks from her white-bread classmates. If Ruby survived school with darker skin, our daughter knows she can, too.

"High school is a faint memory," she lies.

"I remember those days like they were yesterday."

Nodding slowly, a still agitated Ruby puts on a smile for Chevelle. We've hit an impasse. She wants me to shut up, but I've spent years missing her. Once my mouth starts flapping about how amazing Ruby is, I can't stop myself.

TWENTY SIX - RUBY

Elle's soft breathing does nothing to relax me. Instead, it reminds me of how she's sound asleep, and I'm alone with a wide-awake Bonn in the next bed. I feel him thinking and know he's aware I'm thinking, too. I'm sure he worries about his meeting tomorrow. His nerves aren't what I'm focused on, though. I'm more interested in the way my body aches for his touch.

Restless, I roll out of bed and shuffle to the bathroom. I think about taking a cold shower in the hopes of washing away my obnoxious hormones. I also consider helping myself chill, but my clit doesn't want self-stimulation. My throbbing center craves the sexy man in the next room, even if my heart still aches from his long-ago betrayal.

Once hiding in the bathroom loses its allure, I decide to go back to bed and try to sleep. I open the door to find a shirtless Bonn standing on the other side. He steps closer, forcing me to back up. We play this game until he shuts the door and removes my escape route.

"What?" I ask.

"I don't know what'll happen tomorrow. I wanted to tell you something in case things don't work out with the Reapers."

"Are you trying to scare me?"

"This is me being honest like I should have been when we had Chevelle, and I got scared. I want you to know what I'm thinking, so you won't have to guess."

Crossing my arms over my tender nipples, I shrug. "Okay. Say what you need to say."

Bonn's dark gaze roams my face, studying me for nearly a minute before he speaks.

"I still love you. We've changed in some ways, but the core ones remain the same. You're the woman I loved back when you were still a girl. I lost you, and I might never get you back, but I will never stop loving you."

"You're not dying tomorrow," I mutter because no other words are possible without following them with tears.

"I know."

"You'll be fine."

"I know that, too."

"You'll come back here, and we'll go swimming."

Bonn leans down and kisses me. His lips hold back, careful not to take more than I'll give. I wonder how he can control his lust when I'm barely able to keep my clothes on.

As if hearing my thoughts, Bonn wraps a hand around my hip and guides me closer. His lips cover mine while his tongue forces its way inside my mouth. Tasting me elicits a moan from him. Or maybe the moan was from me. I can't think when my entire body has abandoned self-control.

When my fingertips graze his chest, I'm shocked by the heat of his skin. He's on fire, and I'm sure I'll freeze if I can't get closer. Wrapping my arms around his waist, I never want to let go.

His hands find my face, sliding into my hair and pressing my head back so our kiss can deepen. My mind reels under the heat of our need, but my body still isn't satisfied.

My feet shuffle backward while my fingers grip his boxers. I pull him along until my hips bump against the sink. Bonn's lips never leave mine, even as he lifts me up onto the counter. I grip one of his hands immediately and press it between my legs. He needs to know I can't wait. My clit throbs painfully, aching for pleasure only he can provide.

Bonn's fingers move slowly over my hot flesh before dipping between the folds and stroking my tender nub. I nearly come at the feel of his first caress. Kissing him faster, I lift my hips and slide forward until I'm nearly off the counter. My body craves pleasure and finds it when he presses one finger inside me while his thumb makes possessive circles against my clit.

Gasping, I let go of his lips and struggle against my cry of relief. Elle seems so far away, like a ghost from another world. Nothing exists except this moment in this room with this man.

100

Bonn's movements are a blur. My flannel nightgown comes off at one point. His hot lips cover my nipple, claiming it the way his fingers did my pussy. I tease his hair, tugging gently, guiding him to my other breast.

Every sensation is both familiar and shockingly different. We're the same Bonn and Ruby as years ago, yet strangers in too many ways.

My mind recognizes the delicious feel of his hard cock teasing my slit. He wants inside me again after so many years without. My body demands I submit to his desire. Bonn needs me, and I can barely exist without him.

Except my mind can't forget. Like my daughter in the next room, Kim feels far away. Yet, she still exists, and she once knew Bonn in the same way I'm about to know him again.

His lips find mine, and he kisses me harder, faster, begging for an answer to his probing cock between my legs. *Can he reclaim what he lost even if for one night?*

I think of Harmony, a hint of my old life before this heated moment. She said Kim stole my man, and I need to reclaim him. Until I did, I would never truly see Bonn, only what was stolen.

My legs wrap around his waist as my hips tilt backward. I offer my pussy to his thick cock. Distrustful of my currently slumbering temper, I don't say the words. I can't cry out his name in approval. My heart and mind fall silent while my body welcomes him back.

TWENTY SEVEN - BONN

Ruby exhales deeply when my cock enters her body. With every inch, the pink of her cheeks warms. Eyes closed, she's the picture of erotic perfection. *How have I gone so long without witnessing her pleasured expression?* Even worse, how did I think to betray such a divine creature?

We've been apart for too long to take our time finding satisfaction. Like two animals in heat, we move fast and hard together, needing relief from the misery I forced upon us.

Her body breaks out in a sweat when I reach down to tease her clit. I see the hot beads glisten on her skin in the mirror. I watch the way she leans her head to each side and how her dark hair sways against her bare skin.

I want Ruby to come again. I want to taste her on my fingers. I want to devour the flesh now full of my cock. I want everything, and I can hardly wait to come so I can fuck her again.

My fingers tickle down her spine, teasing the bones before I grip her hips with both hands and thrust harder. Though I wish I could spend forever watching Ruby's body in the mirror, I've lasted longer than my balls can tolerate.

Aroused beyond anything I've ever endured, I need to come inside Ruby and reclaim my woman. I don't think of relationships or feelings. I only need to possess her in a way a man owns a woman. Primal and desperate, I need to fuck her forever so no one else can ever know her in this way.

Cupping her breast, I pinch the nipple between my fingers while my other hand wraps around her back to keep her from sliding on the slick countertop.

"Bonn," she moans, biting into my arm to stifle her cries of pleasure.

The hunger in her voice mixes with the pain from her teeth, leaving me a slave to my orgasm. Grunting with satisfaction, I fill her pussy with my seed. Something I had feared as a teenager, I now crave as a man.

I demand Ruby be mine and no one else's. If I could leave a claiming mark on her, I would. Instead, I thrust deeper until Ruby whimpers at the pressure. She never pauses her hips or pushes me away. She craves more pain and pleasure. Every sensation is both too much yet not enough.

Cupping the back of her neck, I wish I could say magical words to fix what I broke. I stare into her dark, pleasured eyes and wish everything were different. That I'd never made her cry or doubt herself. That I hadn't failed our family. That I'd been an honorable man when it counted.

"What now?" she asks, sounding lost in the pleasure still radiating between our bodies.

"Everything," I whisper. "That's what I want and what you need. Just everything."

Ruby stares at me, unable to respond. She's stuck in the basest part of her mind where only carnal needs matter. Tomorrow, she'll remember my sins. For tonight, we can forget.

TWENTY EIGHT - RUBY

After an hour in the bathroom with Bonn, I sleep like the dead. My body feels emptied out in the best way. Leaving Bonn in a hurry, I climbed into bed, afraid to say or do anything that might ruin my satisfying buzz.

Elle *doesn't* sleep like the dead. She wakes up at seven in the same way she does at home. I stir when she climbs out of bed. She sits at the small table and plays on her tablet. Elle nibbles on one of the millions of snacks I brought since I apparently didn't think food existed in Kentucky.

Finally, Bonn's voice wakes me enough to force my butt out of bed. I hear Elle whispering to him about the hotel's free breakfast and how she isn't that hungry, but she would eat a lot if we went. Catching the hint, I drag myself to the shower.

Awake now, I realize the face in the mirror won't win any beauty contests. I'm too tired to care. Well, until I open the bathroom door to find Bonn looking sleepy yet perfect. The expression he wears mimics the one from the night before when he took charge and offered me what I desperately needed.

Staring into his eyes, I remember how full I felt with him inside me. I'd gone far too fucking long without knowing that feeling.

"Good morning," he says, leaning down to kiss me.

Suddenly, I remember something besides dick, pussy, and orgasm. Our daughter is nearby. This man cheated on me with a stupid bitch he claims he didn't even like. Oh, and today he is meeting with the top criminal in these parts.

Stepping back, I press my hand to his chest. "Last night was fun, but I'm not sure what it was beyond that."

"Fun?" he asks, cocking an eyebrow.

"Don't get your panties in a bunch."

"Speaking of panties, when did you start sleeping without them?"

104

Rolling my eyes, I whisper, "Last night happened because I hadn't had sex for so long. I got caught up in the physical stuff, but I'm not okay with the other stuff. Do you get me?"

A smiling Bonn nods. "Oh, I get you, minx."

I start to push past him to find my shoes when an idea pops into my head. Pausing, I whisper, "I'm on the pill. I probably should have mentioned that last night, but my brain wasn't in charge."

"I know the feeling," he says, running his fingers down my spine the way he did when my body was filled with his cock.

"Stop," I whimper, now wanting to fuck so bad I doubt I can walk straight.

"Mom, here are your shoes."

Nothing kills the ache between my legs like the child I shoved out of that region. She smiles at me while handing me my shoes. I return her grin and mentally thank her for throwing cold water on my lust.

We walk downstairs to the breakfast area, where Elle acts like she's at the fanciest place on the planet. She wants everything, though seeming nervous she might embarrass herself in front of the other Holiday Inn Express visitors.

Wearing a satisfied smile, Bonn silently watches us throughout breakfast. I avoid his gaze, unable to deal with my competing emotions. Rather than ponder complicated things like love, forgiveness, and animalistic lust, I focus on our daughter.

"Dad, where are you going today?" Elle asks while we walk back to the room.

"I have a business meeting."

"About what?"

"Boring stuff."

Elle gives him a weird look, and I don't blame her. She thinks he does construction, and that means he builds stuff. When I told her about the trip, she asked if he was making something in Kentucky, and I said no. Elle tends not to ask questions when she worries about the answers.

Once in the room, she crawls onto the bed and stretches out with the remote. I smile at how tall she is already. Sally is five-seven like me, and I suspect Elle will beat us both.

"Can we talk?" Bonn whispers in my ear, startling me from my thoughts.

We stand at the door while Elle finds cartoons to watch.

"I have a stupid question," Bonn says.

"Spill it, and I promise not to point and laugh."

Bonn, wearing a dark blue button-up shirt and black jeans, shakes out his arms and checks himself in the mirror.

"What do I do with my hands?" he asks, in nearly a whisper. "If I stand with my arms relaxed, I look too passive. If I put my hands in my pockets, I seem too casual. If I cross my arms, I come off as aggressive. What's the right way to handle someone like Johansson?"

"The twins are like him."

"Yes, but they've known me since we were kids. I never worry about making a good impression with them."

Studying Bonn, I have an incredible urge to touch his throat and run my fingers south until I hit pay dirt.

"Don't think about how to behave. Men like Johansson spend their time with tough guys and will know when someone's putting on an act. You're not looking to join their club. You don't need to make a good impression. You just need to remember the facts of your plan. He'll decide if it works for him, not based on you but the numbers."

Exhaling slowly, Bonn struggles against his nerves. Seeing his vulnerability freaks me out a little. He hasn't acted this way around me since we first found out I was pregnant, and he thought I'd blame him for having super sperm.

"I've run through what I want to say so many times that it's a mess in my head."

"I know you have a lot riding on today, but you're good under pressure. Every time you had a school presentation, you would get nervous about saying something dumb. Then, you'd stand up and blow everyone away. It was ridiculous how relaxed you got when you were on. You need to trust that'll happen today with Johansson."

His anxious gaze relaxes, leaving behind what I can only assume is a strong interest in seeing me naked soon.

Patting his hand, I step back. "If you plan to work for someone like Hayes, you'll need to handle rough types. Not goofballs like your cousins when they're with you, but the way they are with other rough types. You'll need to walk into a room and feel like you belong. If you can't do that, your big plan won't work. Common Bend is a mess, and you told Hayes you could clean it up. I know you have it in you to be a cold fucker in the right circumstances. Now, you have to prove it to him."

Bonn smiles at my words, but I'm fairly certain he's thinking about how close we're standing in the bathroom. His mind is on last night, and my mind can't help recalling the amazing power of orgasms.

Now isn't the time for a replay of last night's greatest hits. Yet, I offer him a goodbye kiss that promises more if only he'll return safely to Elle and me.

TWENTY NINE - BONN

The Reapers' main office is located between a Thai restaurant and a frozen yogurt shop. Parking across the street from it, I survey the area. Mothers push strollers, and college kids stare at their phones. If not for the Harleys parked in front of the office, I'd think I was in the wrong place.

Inside the office, I find an elderly woman sharpening a pencil until it's a mere stump. She looks up at me before throwing the pencil into the trash.

"May I help you?" she asks, fiddling with her glasses.

"I have an appointment with Mister Johansson."

"Yes. He's finishing up with something important. Please sit down, and I'll ask when he can see you."

I watch the little woman shuffle down a hallway. When she opens a door, I hear the distinct sounds of a pool game in progress.

"Cooper, that man is here," she says.

"Thanks, Bette. I'm about to beat these shitheads. Give me a minute."

The woman shuts the door and shuffles back. She sits in her chair, adjusts herself, looks over her desk, and finally glances up at me.

"He's on a call, but he'll see you soon."

Smiling, I admire her ability to lie so effortlessly. No doubt, Bette was a heartbreaker in her youth and lied to the boys to keep them hanging on.

I check my phone while I wait for Johansson. Earlier, Ruby texted me a thumbs-up. I also find a message from Candy, reminding me about the meeting and how I better not fuck it up. She follows that text with a smiling face. Now, I'm unsure if she's serious about her threat or not.

"Bette, send him back," Johansson says from down the hall.

"You heard him," she says, sharpening another pencil to oblivion.

I walk past her and down the hallway to an office where two men and a woman wait. The older guy has dark hair and light eyes and is probably the muscle. The way he stands next to the dark-haired young woman makes me think they're together.

The guy behind the desk is clearly the boss. While I expect Cooper to be around the twins' age, he seems younger. I wouldn't be surprised if he's only a few years past legal to buy beer. His blond hair has a boyish quality betrayed by his hard, dark eyes.

"Bonn Fletcher," he says, gesturing for me to sit down. "These are my associates, Judd and Tawny. They're sticking around while we talk. Now, let's get to the point because I'm curious as fuck about why you're here."

"Didn't Hayes give you a hint?"

"I talked to his wife, who is a fan of cryptic messages. Apparently, you're a dealmaker, and I'm your newest mark."

Exhaling, I need to thank Candy for prepping Cooper so well. "Hayes wants to buy Common Bend."

Cooper doesn't hide his surprise. Blinking hard, he regains his composure quickly, but I relax knowing he isn't the all-seeing badass I'd imagined.

"Why the fuck would he want Common Bend?"

"So, the Serrated Brotherhood can't have it."

Cooper smiles, but his eyes crackle with anger. "They already can't fucking have it."

"That's not what I hear in Hickory Creek. The current management wants Common Bend."

"Why?"

"Ego shit going back to when your dad took it from them."

"Yeah, they fucking lost it, and they can't have it back."

His anger stalls my confidence. Rather than fearing I've bitten off more than I can handle, I smile at the thought of Ruby. Cooper isn't sure what to make of my grin and watches me warily. I suspect he worries I'll make a move against him. Behind him, Judd stiffens and stands closer to Tawny.

"I'm going to be square with you. Besides your name and that of your club, I don't know shit about you," I say, resting my hands on my lap. "I don't know what you can and can't do, so maybe you want a war with the Brotherhood over a shitty little town. Or possibly you know Common Bend is more work than it's worth, and you want rid of it."

Cooper glances at Judd and then back at me. When he doesn't speak, I continue, "While you might want to be rid of Common Bend, there's no way you want it to end up with the Brotherhood. So, what I need to know is if you're willing to sell it to Hayes?"

"I don't see what's in it for me."

"No offense, but you're doing a real shit job in Common Bend."

"Is that right?" Cooper grumbles.

"How much product is wasted by the dealers before it hits the streets? How many pimps are skimming off the top before they send you the profit? Whoever you have running Common Bend doesn't have a handle on it. That's why Hayes gets nervous. Common Bend's issues bleed into White Horse. The Brotherhood would run it better, but no one wants them expanding north."

"It might not be running smoothly, but the shithole brings us a profit."

"Fine, but how much of that money will be wasted on fighting with the Brotherhood when they make a move?"

"Where the fuck are you hearing they want to move against me? I haven't heard that shit."

"I live in Hickory Creek and know the Rutgers twins," I say and then throw in the info Cooper will care most about. "And my father is Howler Hallstead. So, I hear shit. I know the mood in town. Before Mojo and Howler hand the club over to the twins, they want to take back Common Bend. It's an ego thing, and they'll burn everything down to do it. I mean, they're old as fuck and ready to die anyway. Why not fuck everyone else over while they act out their grudge match?"

Cooper glances again at his people, and I know he's dying to talk to them alone. They want to hash out what I'm saying and figure out if their investments are in trouble. In fact, I wouldn't be surprised if Cooper picks up the phone as soon as I leave and calls his dad for advice.

"What about the twins?"

"I get the impression they don't want Common Bend. Their eyes are on moving south toward Nashville, but they're not calling the shots yet."

Cooper rubs his jaw and sits back in the chair. "What's Hayes offering?"

"A onetime three million payment. You walk away, and he takes control of the town."

"Three million seems low."

"Not based on what dealers and pimps are claiming they send you."

"Those fuckers sure like to chat my business, don't they?" Cooper says, sitting up and looking ready to kick someone's ass.

"I only know rumors, but there's no strong Reapers' presence in Common Bend. The sheriff's office is weak, and they get pushed around by the dealers. I know the last sheriff tried to take over. So, you're stuck with a choice of sending more of your people to run things, empower the sheriff, and hope he doesn't think he's the boss, or leaving things the way they are now. All while waiting to see what crap the Brotherhood pulls."

"Or I can sell it to Hayes."

"You'd get rid of a problem and still stick it to your rivals."

"Can you believe this shit, Judd?" Cooper asks his man.

Even though Cooper's anger pulses through the office, I think of Ruby's hot breath on my neck the night before. If I can make her mine, the rest of my life is a cakewalk.

"Who would run shit for Hayes?" Judd asks from behind Cooper. "He never seemed interested in dipping his big fucking toes in the shithole."

"I would oversee it."

"And who the fuck are you?" Cooper growls. "Your pop is the VP of a club you want to screw over."

111

"Some men want to be like their fathers. Others want to crush their fathers. I won't kill Howler, but I can steal his dream."

"Fucking with the old man is ballsy, so why don't I just hire you to run Common Bend and keep it for the Reapers?"

His question throws me off for a minute. Being unfamiliar with the club, I never considered working for the Reapers. Hitting up Hayes made more sense. Now, I'm temporarily stumped.

Finally, I blurt out, "Because you don't want Common Bend, or you'd send someone down there to run it."

Cooper sighs. "I do fucking hate that town. It's always one problem after another."

"It needs to be micromanaged. The dealers need to be vetted. They either do their jobs or get replaced. Same with the pimps. The sheriff needs to know his place, too. That's a lot of work, and I assume your expansion plans don't involve going south."

"Why not?"

"It puts you on a path toward the Brotherhood, and your backers in Memphis don't want a war. They'll let you fight over Common Bend but never Nashville."

Cooper rubs the back of his neck and stands up. "I hear you're staying at the Holiday Inn."

"Yes," I say, standing slowly.

"Are you in town alone?"

More than once, I've considered how to answer this question if it came up. I always figured honesty was the only option.

"I brought my woman and kid."

Cooper's gaze softens a little. "Look, you came here with an offer I hadn't even considered. I can't sign off on anything without thinking shit out and running the numbers. Why don't you come out to my parents' house tomorrow for lunch? We're grilling, and there'll be kids for yours to play with. Your woman can gossip with our women, and you and I can talk about what I've decided."

Agreeing, I'm already sweating Ruby's reaction. She's wary enough about my meeting the Reapers. No way will she want Chevelle anywhere around them. Her idea of a perfect weekend is spending the entire time at the hotel. It's mine, too, but I need to see this thing through to the end, even if I'm forced to drag Ruby along for the ride.

THIRTY - RUBY

Elle could spend the entire day in the pool, stopping only to eat and use the bathroom. I watch her play with a couple of kids while their mom talks on the phone. My daughter's normally shy. These two boys are younger, so she isn't intimidated.

Restless, I dial Harmony's number and hope we can gossip.

"Well?" Harmony asks rather than saying hello. "Sex is fun, huh?"

"Yes, very much so."

"Can you talk?"

"Yes."

"Can you get disgustingly graphic?"

"Nope. I'm at the pool with Elle."

"Did you do it once or many, many times?"

"More like several times in the bathroom last night."

"So, you couldn't scream for joy, then. Too bad."

"I really needed it. Today, though, I'm thinking about consequences."

"Of course, you are, old lady. It's your way to crap things up with your rational thinking. Damn, I'm glad I don't live in your head."

"Hey," I grumble.

"Sorry. Keanu threw up last night, and I'm cranky. Also, I'm jealous I haven't enjoyed a porking in a while."

"Is he okay?"

"Sure. He puked, watched TV, puked more, and fell asleep. I was the one who cleaned things up and worried all night. Kids have it so easy. I miss being three and carefree."

"You are tired."

"Yeah, but I'm joyfully happy for you. Bonn too. I'm sure his penis is the most joyfully happy of us all."

"Oh, I'm sure it threw a party with his balls after we were done. Lots of high-fiving and reminiscing."

"Now what?"

"I have no clue. More fun tonight before we drive back. Then, the real world will smother my joy."

"Oh, please stop with your optimism. It's nauseating."

Grinning, I wave at Elle, who shows me another trick. "Have you heard from Daisy?"

"Of course. She calls me every day to say how great marriage is and how Camden's giant penis hasn't killed her yet."

"Did you tell her anything?"

"I told her I was happy she survived another night with the giant penis."

Snorting, I roll my eyes. "No, I meant about me."

"I said I would keep your secret, so stop your nagging."

"What I'm about to say comes from love, okay? After we hang up, Harmony, you need to take a nap before you piss off someone standing close enough to slap you."

"Okay, Mom. While I nap, you make sure to save your energy for tonight's debauchery."

"Will do."

Harmony yawns, making me need to do the same. Once we finish, she sighs.

"I want the best for you, Ruby," Harmony says in a sleepy voice. "Try to have fun and leave the serious stuff for later."

"I will, sis. I miss you."

"Miss you, too. We'll share all the dirty details when you get back."

Hanging up, I try to get comfortable in the uncomfortable lawn chair. Soon, my mind shifts to Bonn and his meeting. I don't know how worried I should be. I grew up with the Serrated Brotherhood Motorcycle Club. They're scary because they could kill me without losing a night's sleep. Of course, I also know they won't because I'm not a threat to them.

The Brotherhood is a terrifying, familiar threat, but the Reapers are just scary. What if Johansson decides to hurt or kill Bonn to make a point? No one would stop him, and I can't imagine even the Rutgers twins going to war over one death.

Bonn is replaceable to the powers running the criminal trifecta of Common Bend, Hickory Creek Township, and White Horse. For Elle, he's the person who helps her dream. I'm her rock, but Bonn makes her feel like a princess in a world of trailer parks and low-rent jobs.

I'm not sure what Bonn represents for me. *Is he the past I can't let go of or the present I hope to build on?* Can I ever look at him without seeing Kim Crawley?

When he appears at the pool door, a few of my questions are answered immediately. He looks healthy, with not a hair out of place. I also don't even remember Kim exists as I sigh with relief and join him.

"How did it go?" I ask, unsure if I should hug him.

A grinning Bonn takes my outstretched hand and shakes it. "Nice to meet you."

Rolling my eyes, I yank my hand free. "I'm nervous."

Bonn glances at the kids in the pool and smiles for Elle. She waves at him before bouncing in the water.

"How did it go?"

"Okay, but I don't have an answer yet."

"Did he seem interested?"

"I couldn't tell. He mostly seemed surprised by the issues I mentioned in Common Bend. They really don't keep a good eye on the town."

I finally get up the courage to rest my hand on his chest. Bonn glances down at where I lightly touch him. His gaze finds my face, and he lifts an eyebrow.

"Oh, stop," I mutter, removing my hand. "Not everything has to mean something."

"Sometimes, everything *does* mean something," he says, seizing my hand before I can flee. Bonn kisses my palm before pinning it to his chest. "Whenever I got nervous, I thought of you to relax."

Bonn's deep tone makes me think of our time together in the bathroom. Every time he said my name last night, his voice rumbled with need. Now, he's doing the same thing, but we're in no position to act on our desires.

"I'll meet you later in our rendezvous spot," I say, stepping back and reclaiming my hand. "You know the one."

116

"Yes, it has the best view."

"Funny."

Before I return to my seat, Bonn wraps his arms around my shoulders and holds me from behind.

"I agreed to something you won't like."

My entire body tenses and I'm ready to slap him without even knowing why.

"Do they want you to strip for them?" I growl, wondering if he plans to party with the bikers and their club whores.

Bonn leans down and nips my lobe. "You're so temperamental. Is that something new you came up with in the last nine years?"

"I'm going to hurt you," I hiss, trying to pull free.

"Johansson invited us to his family's house tomorrow. They'll grill, and you'll gossip. Chevelle will play with other kids. I'll do manly things like make business deals and chop wood."

Turning around in his arms, I study his relaxed face. "Is that it?"

"Yes."

"Oh."

"You're giving in that easily?"

"Do you want me to fight you?"

"No. I want you to give me everything my heart desires, but we both know that's not how this works."

"No, it's not. But if Johansson has his family around, he probably won't whack you."

"I don't see why he would want to do that anyway. I'm no threat to him, and I don't sense he kills for the fun of it."

I glance back at Elle. "As long as she doesn't know what kind of people they are, I think it'll be okay. She thinks the twins are funny and nice, and we both know that's not true."

"Oh, I don't know. They're pretty funny when they want to be."

"I meant the nice thing."

"They're nice to her, and that's all that matters to a child. I'm sure Johansson only invited me because he needs

117

more time to figure out his decision. This way, he can act like a good host while also talking things out with his dad."

I study Bonn's expression, finding him relaxed in a way he shouldn't be after a tension-filled meeting.

"Do you feel you can make this thing work alone? Johansson has his father and club. Hayes has his wife and whoever he pays to beat up his enemies. The twins have the club and the Hallstead family. You're doing this all alone with no backup."

"Down the road, when the twins run the Brotherhood, we'll work well together. I think Hayes can be trusted as long as he gets what he wants."

"What about right now?"

"I have you."

"I can't do anything to help you," I say, sounding scared.

"You gave me the pep talk this morning."

"That's not much."

"It's more than I have alone."

"It's not enough."

"It's worth more than you can know, Ruby."

"I wasn't enough to make you strong when you were scared to be a father. How can I be enough when you're facing men like Johansson and Hayes? Or when you're making an enemy of your father?"

Bonn frowns before shaking his head. "It was never that you weren't enough. I was afraid to show you my fear. I didn't think you'd want me if you saw how small I felt. That was my failure, not yours. Now, I realize you've seen me at my worst and still find value in me. You can't know how powerful that is."

I'm not sure what Bonn sees in my eyes, but I pray I can live up to what he needs. Putting aside my anger and resentment, I refuse the failure to be on me if this second chance goes down in flames.

THIRTY ONE - BONN

After a day of swimming, Chevelle crashes by nine. I sit in the hotel chair and study her face illuminated by only the TV's light. Nearby, Ruby stares at the flashing screen, but I suspect she isn't watching the show.

Not long after Chevelle begins quietly snoring, Ruby and I find ourselves standing in the bathroom. She looks tiny in her oversized flannel nightgown. Without thinking, I reach out to fix the inside-out collar. Ruby flinches at the feel of my fingers against her bare neck.

Her gaze scans the bathroom before finding me. I'm startled by the sadness in her eyes.

"I guess my lust last night blinded me to how the bathroom isn't very romantic."

"It's true that I never imagined we'd rekindle things this way."

Ruby sighs. "I don't know what I want."

Stepping closer, I cup her jaw. "I think you do, but what you want is scary."

"I haven't been reckless since Elle was born, and trusting you feels reckless to me."

"Nothing I say will make you feel any different. Only my actions can change your mind about trusting me."

Ruby leans into my hand, still caressing her face. "I'm so tired tonight."

"Do you want me to let you sleep?"

"No. I need to be close," she says and then whispers, "Even if it's a lie."

I lift her onto the sink and press her against my chest. Wrapped in my arms, Ruby relaxes.

"In one night, I destroyed everything we had. I'll need more than one night to fix it. If you can give me the time to prove to you that I'm the man you need, I promise we can be happy again."

Ruby lifts her head from my chest and studies me. "You can kiss me now."

119

"There's no hurry. I should probably hold you for a while longer."

"Are you screwing with me?"

"Don't you like sitting bare-assed on the cold countertop?" I ask, smirking.

"What makes you think it's cold?" she asks, mimicking my smile. "I've been thinking about you fucking me since we got back to the room. That's a lot of heat built up between my legs. Hell, I'm surprised the countertop isn't sizzling."

"Are you begging to be fucked?" I whisper while yanking off my plain white T-shirt. "Is that what you need from me?"

"I won't beg."

"You're begging a little."

Ruby scoots back and lifts her legs until her feet rest on the countertop. Now, I have a wonderful view of how much she's been thinking about me.

"I'll never beg," she murmurs as her fingers open her soft folds to reveal wet flesh. "I'll never ask for anything. I'm too self-sufficient."

Ruby proves how capable she is when her index finger teases her swollen clit. Closing her eyes, she makes me feel like a third wheel. I struggle against the terrible urge to leave her alone to satisfy herself. *How long before she stormed after me and demanded to be serviced?* I'd give her about ten minutes before she'd decide I needed to pick up the slack.

As much as I would like to force a little begging from Ruby, I can't leave this room. My gaze locks on her pussy. I haven't tasted it for so long, and I'm a starving man. Last night, we couldn't stop fucking long enough for me to eat her out. Seeing my opportunity, I yank my cock out of my boxers and kneel in front of her.

Never so thankful to be tall, I inhale the scent of her pussy only inches from my licking lips. Ruby opens her eyes a crack and smiles down at me. She pulls back her nightgown to show me her nipple that she squeezes into a hard knot.

120

"I want *you* to beg," Ruby purrs before closing her legs when I lean forward. "Look at how you're already on your knees."

"Please, baby," I murmur. "Let me taste your pussy. Please, let me suck on your clit and fuck you with my tongue. I'm so hungry, and I know you'll taste so fucking good."

Ruby's finger on her clit moves faster, and I swear she's about to come from hearing my words.

My hands slide down her legs and press open her thighs so I can see her pussy convulse. Wrapping my arms around her waist, I tug her forward so I can lick the slick flesh. Ruby moans as my tongue and her finger work together to break down her worries until only pleasure remains.

THIRTY TWO - RUBY

An orgasm is magic, washing away the pain and fear from my sane mind.

Even with the hard countertop under me, and the awkwardness of having Elle in the next room, I find myself in a state of uncontrollable heat. *How did I survive for so long without this kind of pleasure?*

As he devours my flesh, I replay his words. The way his voice rumbled when he begged to taste my most private spot. I remember our first time at oral sex was like, but those days were a million years ago. Even yesterday feels so distant. Everything before the point where he laps up my juices is a quaint memory from a different lifetime.

Bonn makes my body hum before his tongue even fucks me. Pressing deeper, he isn't satisfied and tugs me closer, wanting more. My hips gyrate frantically against his lips. So close to another orgasm, I'm lost in anticipation. Wiggling wildly, I finally give Bonn want he craves.

"Please," I beg while he pumps his tongue into my body. "Please, Bonn."

His lips latch onto my painfully tender clit and suck, making me come so hard that I nearly jump off the countertop. The pleasure and pain of his merciless sucking leave me out of breath and unsure if I alerted the entire hotel about my orgasm.

"I'm fucking you," he growls, grabbing me by the throat and pulling me closer for a wet kiss.

Tasting my pleasure on his tongue, I scoot forward and seek out his cock. I hear him fisting it. The sound of his flesh slapping together elicits a moan from me. I want what his hand now enjoys. I need him to stretch me open and make me beg again.

"Bonn," I groan when he flicks my clit with the head of his cock. "Please."

"Beg more," he demands, using my inflamed clit to tease the slit of his cock. "Tell me you belong to me."

"I'm yours."

"Only mine."

"No one else."

"You wanted to fuck that guy from the restaurant."

"No."

"You smiled at him."

"I was faking," I whimper as the pressure on my clit brings me closer to another orgasm. "He wasn't you. I only want you."

Bonn forces me to look into his eyes. "No one else will ever know your body."

"No one else."

Shoving his cock into me with one violent thrust, Bonn claims my body, and I'm lost in another orgasm. I grip his shoulders and rock my hips violently with the waves of pleasure.

"My heart was yours the moment we met," he gasps, fucking me so hard he needs to hold my hips still to keep me from sliding off the countertop. "How could I touch anyone else?"

Beneath my animalistic hunger, I hear his voice cracking. I might feel tears against my cheek as he empties himself inside me. Bonn broke *his* heart years ago, too, and he's desperate to heal.

Wrapping him in my arms, I want to forgive him. If only, so I can find more pleasure at his touch. Every nerve in my body is focused on coming again. I don't care about anything beyond keeping him with me for another hour or two.

Tomorrow, I might be black and blue from fucking so hard in a room not meant for screwing. I'll worry about the consequences then. For right now, we're two bodies reaching for redemption with every thrust.

THIRTY THREE - BONN

I guess I'm getting old. My dick eventually begs for a time-out. Ignoring its complaints, I refuse to remove the limp flesh from Ruby's still sucking pussy. My heart fears if my arms let her go again—even for a few hours to sleep–I might never have her in them again. Losing her nearly destroyed me, and I can't go through the pain again.

Ruby eventually slides off the countertop and kneels to return my boxers to my hips. She finds her nightgown and slides it over her head. Taking my hand, she guides me to the room where Chevelle still snores.

Rather than climb into her bed, Ruby slides under my blankets. I nearly dive next to her, ready to giggle like a fucking kid at having her with me longer.

"I don't want Elle waking up with us like this," Ruby whispers. "She'll get ideas that we don't need her thinking."

"I love you," I say because no other words matter.

Ruby watches me in the darkness. Her eyelids are heavy, and she needs rest. Yet, Ruby refuses to sleep. She only considers whether she can admit she loves me, too.

"Tomorrow," I murmur, kissing her forehead and providing an out for her dilemma.

Ruby caresses my jaw, running her fingers over my facial growth. She remains silent for so long that I don't think she'll speak.

"Loving you doesn't fix anything," she says, and I hear a hint of anger in her voice. "But I do love you, Bonn. I always have, and I always will."

Kissing her cheek, followed by her pouty lips, I replay her words in my head. *Let her be angry for a million years as long as her heart only belongs to me.*

"Tomorrow," I say again. "I'll fix things. And the next day and the next. I'll make things better for the rest of our lives."

Even in the mostly dark room, I catch Ruby smiling slightly. She nuzzles her lips against my bare chest before exhaling deeply and finally sleeping.

For hours after she dozes off, I remain awake. My scrambled thoughts keep me wondering about our future. I'm also sweating the meeting at Johansson's place. I suspect he'll agree to my plan, which is only the first step in the long process to improve my family's prospects. I'll juggle as many dangerous problems as necessary if happiness for Ruby and Chevelle are my rewards.

THIRTY FOUR - RUBY

I get lucky when Elle wakes up uncharacteristically late, leaving me enough time to crawl out of Bonn's bed before she catches us. Sleepy-eyed and a little congested, my baby cuddles next to me in the same way she did as a toddler.

Back then, Elle didn't handle switching homes well. Each time she returned from a weekend with Bonn, she clung to me and asked every ten minutes where he was.

Even now, Elle craves us in one place. I'd love to tell her we'll be a family living together, but two days of fun in a hotel doesn't translate to forever. I do love Bonn, and I always will, but truly trusting him is another matter.

As he sleeps, I take a shower and wash off my fatigue along with the stickiness left behind from our union. I'm relieved I trimmed back the hedges between my legs. Last night, Bonn devoured the flesh, leaving me tender. I even catch sight of a hickey on my upper thigh.

Smiling at how thoroughly pleasured my body feels, I can forget the little things waiting for me outside this bathroom. Minor issues like having lunch with killers whose biggest question might be whether to give us separate graves or have us share.

Bonn is awake when I leave the bathroom. He and Elle sit on the edge of his bed, talking about who we'll meet today. She's nervous about new people. I don't blame her. She's spent her entire life in one tiny part of the world so that even this small town in Kentucky overwhelms her.

Seeing me out of the bathroom, Bonn stands and makes his way toward the toilet. I almost expect him to give me a morning kiss, but he only smiles and mumbles hello.

I'm admittedly disappointed by his lack of trying to irritate me with a sloppy welcome. I'd have told him to stop since Elle doesn't need to see us together. But I still wanted him to try.

Using my hand to cover my pouting mouth, I warn myself about acting like a bummed teenage girl. Bonn

126

understands we can't make out in front of our daughter. He's behaving maturely, so I need to do the same. *Yes, that's the truth bomb.* Accept it and move on.

I hear the shower start in the bathroom while I fix Elle's hair. My mind instantly imagines the hot water over Bonn's hard body.

"What's wrong, Mom?" Elle asks, touching my face.

"Huh?"

"Your face got red. Are you sick?"

"No," I say, trying not to laugh at my ridiculous lust-based stupidity. "I'm hungry."

Elle lets my lie go. The trip is wearing her out, and I'm certain she's homesick. I slide on my shoes and brush my hair, all while struggling to keep from imagining Bonn naked. Though his shower only lasts a few minutes before he emerges from the steamy room, I feel as if I've waited hours to see him again.

I glance back at Bonn, feigning a casual smile I don't feel. He walks to me and runs his hand down my back. Even startled by the affection, I still prepare to give him my disapproving frown. Then, he plants a kiss on my lips, shutting down my urge to do more than melt.

If Elle weren't sitting a few feet away, watching us with childlike excitement, I'd shove Bonn onto the bed and ride him for an hour or two. The idea of having the comfort of a bed while we explore sounds too tempting, but I am very aware of our daughter's presence.

Bonn likely is, too. His passionate kiss proves to be a short one. Maybe too short since my fingers cling to his shirt, unwilling to let him go yet.

"Are you ready for breakfast?" Bonn asks Elle.

Our daughter takes his outstretched hand. They walk to the door and wait for me to get my head out of my crotch long enough to follow. I wish I could get rid of the lust clouding my brain and focus on whether I can forgive Bonn. Instead, I crave the blinded bliss that comes from pleasure after too long without.

THIRTY FIVE - BONN

Johansson has me drive out to his parents' property. I don't know why I expect the place to seem like one of those white power compounds with armed men at the entrance. Though I'm familiar with the Brotherhood's setup, the Reapers Motorcycle Club is an entirely different beast.

Ruby is completely silent as soon as we enter the car. She drinks in our surroundings during the drive. In the back seat, Chevelle watches her tablet to keep her mind off meeting new people. We're an SUV full of tension by the time I turn down a long road leading from the highway to the Johansson property.

"That's a big house," Chevelle says, leaning into the front. "Are they rich?"

"Maybe."

Chevelle and Ruby share an awkward smile while I park the SUV in a large gravel lot near the main garage.

"I can smell the grilling meat," I tell them when they stare at me.

"Do you think they'll have a problem with us?" Ruby asks.

I frown, not understanding. She glances at the people drinking nearby on a deck. Her gaze returns to me and gets wide as if hoping I'll catch the hint. *Of course, I don't.*

"People around here seem to like to tan, and we don't," she says slowly and pats her skin before gesturing toward a confused Chevelle.

"Oh, yeah," I say, relieved she didn't need to spell out her concern. "I don't know, but I think it'll be fine. If not, we leave. There are plenty of other places to eat lunch."

Ruby smiles at the sound of my stern tone. She likes when I pull the protective man routine. For a woman normally in charge, she's desperate for someone else to call the shots occasionally.

"We ready?" I ask, smiling at Chevelle.

"Do I have to talk to people?"

"You don't have to do anything, baby," Ruby says immediately.

Still nervous, Chevelle climbs out when I open her door. Her hand reaches for mine and then her mother's. We walk to the front door like a family on a casual trip to the zoo rather than meeting a biker club for barbecue.

Cooper answers the door with a brunette, pigtail-wearing toddler on his hip. A young dark-haired woman stands next to him, cradling a blonde baby girl.

"Didn't know if you'd show," Cooper says.

"Why would I say no to free food?"

Cooper gives me a smile and then glances at the kid he's holding. He wants me to know my family is safe. After all, no one kills people with their kids in tow.

After introducing Ruby and Chevelle, he shows off his wife, Farah, and their kids, Lily and Miranda. Then, we enter the house and meet too many people to remember. I do pay special attention to his father, Kirk. The older version of Cooper offers no signals over his feelings toward me or the deal.

Farah takes Ruby and Chevelle outside to where more women wait with more kids. I sense my woman isn't thrilled to leave me, but she plays along.

"They'll be fine," Cooper says, patting me hard on the back. "Let's talk business before we eat."

I take heart in how he expects me to be alive and hungry after the business conversation. Following him outside, we pass a dozen tattooed men who watch me intently. I'd feel more on the spot if I hadn't spent the last year shaking my ass for sloppy-drunk women.

Cooper and I sit on a quiet side deck where he hands me a beer.

"Three million is too low," Cooper says immediately. "Your numbers are off by a few million."

"What's a few?"

"Two."

Nodding, I study Cooper as if considering his words, but I already knew he'd want more. That's why I got Hayes to agree to seven.

"If he says yes to five million, you'll hand over Common Bend and walk away?"

"You aren't wrong that I have plans that don't involve that shithole. If my pop hadn't fought to keep Common Bend, I'd let the assholes in the Brotherhood take it. This way works for me."

"Let me make a call and get your answer."

Once Cooper gives me a curt nod, I stand up and walk to where I can make a private call.

"It's the weekend," Candy says, answering.

"Tell Hayes five million."

"I don't know who that is."

"Cookie, we should set up a playdate between your twins and my daughter. Spending time with them will help her self-esteem."

"Classy, stripper boy. So, you having fun in Hickland USA?"

"It's nice here. The blondes know how to keep their big mouths shut."

"Nothing sadder than a whipped woman."

"Well, we've been on the phone for long enough to make this look real. Tell your boss what I said whenever it suits you, and I wasn't kidding about the playdate. Chevelle needs to meet people outside of Hickory Creek."

"I'm sure your kid is a cutie. Though I'd bet Ruby ought to take the credit for that."

"I'm hanging up now."

"You do that, and good luck not getting killed."

Hanging up, I walk back to Cooper.

"Well?" he asks, looking bored.

"After saying fuck a few million times, he agreed to your price."

"You're not going to negotiate?"

"He doesn't want to waste more time on Common Bend than he has to."

"Sounds about right."

Cooper stands up and scratches his jaw. "You've got a pretty daughter. She seems shy."

I follow him to where men stand at a line of grills. I spot burgers, hot dogs, steak, and even fat pork chops. Though still tense, I'm too much of a man not to be impressed with so much meat.

"She is," I say, forcing my gaze from the food. "Chevelle gets nervous in new situations."

"Then she must be freaking today."

"Probably. Do you know where they went?"

"She's cool, man," he says, patting my back again. "Let the girls gossip while we eat and talk shit about the Brotherhood."

Cooper hands me a plate full of meat and another beer, even though I haven't finished the first one. I get the distinct impression he's trying to get me drunk so he can pump me for info on his rivals. What he doesn't realize is I don't know shit. However, I won't say no to free steak and beer.

THIRTY SIX - RUBY

Farah and her friends are obnoxious in the same way I am with my sisters. They speak about people I'll never meet and share lots of inside jokes. Their conversations feel hyphenated because they don't need to spell things out to people who know them so well.

I stand there, resenting them and mentally apologizing to all the people who listened to me with Daisy and Harmony. Of course, I won't stop acting the same way in the future. Having a clique is too damn tempting to give up.

Farah's sister, Tawny, brings me food and drink. She's helpful but wary. I'm an outsider surrounded by a tight-knit community of people. I make chit-chat about kids and the difference between Kentucky and Tennessee weather. I'm friendly, but I can't break through their protective shells any more than they could with the people of Lush Gardens and me.

Chevelle left earlier to play with Cooper's little sister, his niece, and a family friend. I watch them walking around the grassy area near a trampoline and pathways. Then, during my conversation about the weather, Chevelle leaves the other kids and returns to me.

"What's wrong?" I ask.

Uneasy with so many eyes on her, Elle lowers her gaze.

"Sawyer was probably a jerk," mutters Cooper's other blonde sister, Bailey. "She's awful. We all hate her."

"I don't hate her," Farah immediately says.

"Yeah, but you're brain-dead from popping out two babies in a year."

"Bailey," Tawny growls, stepping protectively in front of her sister.

Ignoring their mostly mock-tiff, I kneel next to Elle. "Are you okay?"

"She was bossy," Elle whispers. "I don't want to play with them anymore."

"That's okay. You can play with me. Oh, wait, I'm bossy, too."

Elle giggles. "You are not."

"Liar."

I look at the women who now enjoy the happiest argument I've witnessed since Daisy accused Harmony of getting pregnant by Big Foot.

"Could we use your trampoline?" I ask Farah.

"Of course," she says, bouncing her infant before leaning toward Elle. "Sawyer doesn't mean any harm. She's just... Umm, what's a nice way to say bossy?"

"She's a brat," Bailey clarifies. "Just a horrible demon."

Farah frowns at Bailey, who laughs and runs off to torment her much younger sister.

"Don't ask," Farah says. "You can jump or swim or whatever you guys want. Just have fun."

I leave the teasing women to walk down the long line of steps to the yard. Elle holds my hand like we're in danger, and I think she might break a finger.

"What if we fall?" Elle asks, standing in front of the trampoline.

I run my fingers over the protective netting. "That's what this is for." Kicking off my shoes, I look at the ladder. "I want to jump."

Climbing onto the trampoline, I hold a hand out for Elle. She's slower than molasses about removing her shoes and climbing. Eventually, we stand together.

"Let's bounce," I say, holding both of her hands.

Elle looks ready to cry. I don't know why she gets so overwhelmed. Yet, the last few days have clearly worn her down.

"Baby," I softly say while beginning to bounce us. "I'm glad your dad asked us to come on this trip."

A smile warms her face, and I jump a little higher. Elle grips my hands, even while helping me get more lift to our bounces. Soon, our ponytails fly high, and we're both crazy laughing. I never realized how much fun jumping could be. No wonder my daughter bounces through life.

133

While in the air, I catch sight of Bonn watching us from an upper deck. Even with the distance, I know he's smiling. Our joy is his. Bonn loves so easily, and I want to be more like him. I wish I could let go of our painful past and embrace the happiness he now offers.

THIRTY SEVEN - BONN

I'm three beers and two steaks into dinner when Cooper realizes I have zero useful gossip about the Brotherhood. I watch his dark eyes shift from wary friendliness to normal guy bullshitting. I'm now a guest at his parents' place rather than someone he can squeeze for juicy details.

Soon, he and his brother, Tucker, start wrestling on the deck and end up on the ground below. I'd be worried if their mother wasn't chanting her approval. I watch them casually beat on each other and feel good about never having a brother I loved enough to playfully abuse.

"You're Howler's kid," Kirk says, joining me at the railing.

Nodding, I glance down at where Cooper now shoves Tucker's face into a puddle. Nearby, dogs bark excitedly. Farther off in the yard, I see Ruby and Chevelle jumping on the trampoline. I don't think they've ever looked as beautiful to me.

"I knew your dad back in the day."

"If you've spoken to him more than twice, you've got one up on me."

Smirking, Kirk lights a cigarette. "He's shit for sure. Reminded me of my dad. The life of the fucking party, but an asshole the rest of the damn time. Does that sound about right?"

"Yeah. I don't think about him much."

"You thought about him enough to want to piss him off."

"He's one of the reasons I got involved, but not the main concern. That would be the two beauties jumping on your trampoline."

Kirk glances at where Ruby and Chevelle now do splits during every jump. He smiles and exhales cigarette smoke into the hot day.

"I don't want to play pop to you, but I'm gonna give you a bit of advice. That anger you have for Howler is a

135

good motivation. Don't let people tell you otherwise. Anger will get you through the tough times when thinking happy fucking thoughts about family and friends won't do it. Just don't let the anger eat you up until it's all you got left. I know too many good men ruined by their resentments. You seem to have a solid thing with your woman and daughter. You also have a fucking asshole for a father who will come at you with his bullshit the second he learns you fucked him. Gotta weigh those two things when he pushes your buttons because he fucking will."

"I'd be lying if I said I wasn't looking forward to it."

Kirk chuckles. "I wanted to hunt my dad down and crush him long after he was dead. Only thing that saved me was Jodi and the kids. Made me a better man, but I still think of my pop from time to time, and I still want to fuck him up. He's rotted down to the bone now, but it's not enough. Don't be surprised if your revenge against Howler doesn't make you feel much better."

Stretching, Kirk grins down at where Cooper and Tucker now sit on the ground, talking about something casual as if they hadn't been beating on each other minutes earlier.

"That's the end of my speech. Who'd have thought retirement would turn me into a know-it-all, walking around telling people how to live their fucking lives?"

"You built something big here," I say, again watching Ruby and Chevelle. "If anyone ought to be handing out advice, it's a guy who won."

"Good luck with your pop. Hope you don't kill the fucker. Or if you do, that you bury the body nice and deep."

Kirk leaves my side, so he can hassle his muddy sons. Around me, people laugh and enjoy the hot Sunday. I walk down the stairs to the yard where Ruby and Chevelle now softly bounce while holding hands.

"Think this thing can handle one more?" I ask, smiling up at them.

"Yes!" Chevelle cries, immediately crawling toward me. "Mom and I were jumping so high."

"I saw that, but I bet I can beat you both."

136

Ruby grins at me. "Men are so competitive."

"Let me prove your point," I murmur, kicking off my boots and climbing on the trampoline.

Once I stand up, Chevelle takes one of my hands while Ruby reaches for the other. My two beauties begin bouncing, and I follow their tempo until we're flying a foot off the ground. Hearing their laughter, I know they're worth every risk I face with this deal.

THIRTY EIGHT - RUBY

Deep inside, beneath my lust and anxiety about the trip, I prayed the Reapers would reject Bonn's plan. I imagined him feeling like shit for a short time before accepting a less dangerous option. Never did I think a motorcycle club would sell a town. My lack of imagination leaves me shellshocked during the ride back to Hickory Creek Township.

Bonn doesn't say a lot during the drive, and Elle dozes frequently. We're worn out after less than three days away from home. *How can we handle the changes Bonn has in store for us?*

His big plans sound impossible. Panicked now, I only want to return to my trailer, crawl into my lumpy bed, and sleep to the sounds of my neighbor's little dog yapping. I crave boring, ordinary, and safe. My dreams were never big—marrying Bonn, bartending at a decent place, and raising my two kids near my sisters and mother. *Why would I want anything more?*

Bonn's dreams are too big and terrifying for my tastes. After this weekend, we're linked. His dreams mold my future, and there's nothing I can do to change this fact.

I peek at him through my dark hair while he drives to the sounds of the Eurythmics playing quietly on the radio. I've resented Bonn for longer than we were together, yet I can't let him go. He's my ideal, and no other man will satisfy.

Now living apart feels wrong. Bonn and I have a second chance, and he isn't the same eighteen-year-old who broke my heart. He's stronger and smarter. No man could be a better father to Elle or partner to me.

Bonn is my dream, and I won't lose him to a terrifying plan he created to prove something everyone who matters already knows.

THIRTY NINE - BONN

Ruby closes herself off from me during the drive back to Hickory Creek Township. I can't tell what she's thinking or feeling, and not knowing is driving me nuts. Though I never expected having sex would magically fix a pain festering for so many years, I didn't think she'd shut off her heart so suddenly.

We arrive home later than I intend, leaving Ruby in a bad mood as she hurries to get things ready for Chevelle to return to school tomorrow. I help with what she allows but mostly feel like an unwanted third wheel. Even so, I don't leave even after I tuck Chevelle into bed.

Ruby sits on the couch when I walk out of our daughter's room. I stand awkwardly, watching her and wondering if I should bail like she wants. The thought of sleeping alone makes my chest hurt. I can't imagine spending the night at the condo after a weekend with my favorite people.

I join Ruby on the couch, where she pretends to watch the nearly silent TV.

"Are you rethinking things?" I ask when she stares at her hands for too long. "Rethinking us?"

"What if I was?"

"I'd work my charms, so you'd rethink rethinking."

Ruby sighs. "Oh, yeah, your charms."

"What's wrong?"

"Nothing."

"Don't lie to me. You've been acting strange since we left Kentucky."

Ruby's dark eyes take in my face, studying me for a long time before she finds the words. "I want you to back out of this deal."

"What?" I ask, startled and misreading her mood.

"I know I should have said this before, but I wasn't thinking. Not really. When you asked me to go on the trip, I had a moment where I worried about your plan. Mostly, though, I stressed spending time alone with you and how I hadn't traveled with Elle before. I worried about packing and if I'd sleep okay in a strange bed. On the trip, I worried about wanting you and if I would want you the same way when we got back. All that time, I never really thought about what you were doing with Hayes."

Carefully taking her hand, I'm wary of spooking a woman already on edge. "I know this idea is dangerous, but we can make a better life for Chevelle and us. We can give her more than we had growing up."

"I know, but I don't care. Sure, I think about living in a house or how I wish I could take Elle to Dollywood. None of that stuff matters. If you get a regular job and live here with us, we'd be happy. All we need is to be together. The money sounds nice, but it's not worth you getting hurt or killed over. Elle would rather be poor than fatherless."

"It'll be okay, Ruby."

"No."

"I can't back out of this now," I say, hearing a stubborn edge in my tone. "It's too late."

"No, it's not. You can talk to Hayes. Tell him to get someone else to run Common Bend."

"But it was my idea. I've done all the legwork. Why should I let someone else reap the benefits?"

"There's more work to do, though. You have to organize a bunch of violent assholes in Common Bend. Do you think they'll behave because you have good ideas? They'll lash out. Whatever the benefits, losing you won't be worth it."

"I can't walk away," I say, still holding her hand in mine.

"Fine, but then admit you're not doing this for Elle and me. You're doing this to fuck with your dad and prove you're better than JJ or whatever new bastard son shows up. This is about your ego. Can you admit that much?"

Her words hit me hard because they're not wrong. Being a nice guy doesn't mean I don't have a temper or hold a grudge.

"Okay, Ruby. Some of it is ego. But not just about my dad. It's about feeling like I'm a real man who does right by his family. I want to give you a safe home, and I want Chevelle to go to good schools. I want her to have shit I didn't have. That's ego, too, because I grew up with a father who didn't care if I lived or died. I want Chevelle to have everything. That's how I make it up to the kid I used to be. The way I don't resent my shitty childhood is I make sure Chevelle never wants for anything."

Ruby tries to pull her hand free, but I don't give it up. Irritated, she growls, "You'll make her weep over her dead father."

"Hayes has a family and does what he does. Camden too. Mojo had a wife and kids. Why can everyone else have it all while I'm forced to live small?"

"So, living with me and Elle would be small?"

"Don't make this about you not being enough," I mutter, resenting how easily she pulls the guilt card. "And don't pretend I shouldn't want things I don't have. You want them, too. But you've pushed those wants down deep so you can give up everything for our daughter. You gave up trying to find another bartending job because it was better for her if you worked during the day."

"I sacrifice for her."

"And I do, too. But how many times do people like us get a shot at something big? It never fucking happens. The only way I would move up in this world was to grovel at my father's feet. He'd own my happiness. With my plan, I'm free in a way I can't be otherwise."

"Hayes will own your happiness."

"He doesn't want a bitch. All he wants is for trouble to stay away from his precious fucking White Horse. If I do what I need to do, he'll forget I even exist."

"You're naïve," she says, still hoping to win even though I see her accepting our situation.

"I'm dreaming bigger than stripping until I get old or gain a few pounds. Sure, I could probably find a better job for my skills if I left town, but this is where my family lives. My mother and your mother and sisters. This is our home,

141

and I can almost taste my dream coming true. I know you think I'm an arrogant fucker. Stupid too, probably, but I'm so close to making this happen that I can't let it go."

"Even if I threaten to leave you?" Ruby asks with some challenge remaining in her gaze.

"Especially if you threaten. If you want to leave me, I'll feel like less than a man. This job will give me back some of my damn confidence."

"What if the job changes you?"

"I'm a grown man. I won't change much one way or another."

"So, this is the best you can be?" she balks.

I'm hurt by her words until she looks away. Then, I realize she's struggling against laughter.

"Your face," she says, giggling.

"Low blow."

"I want to win this argument, but you won't give in."

"So, you go low?" I grumble.

"I considered using sex to control you. Unfortunately, so long without fucking has made me too needy to use it as a weapon."

"Poor Ruby."

Smiling, she strokes my hand. "I'm scared you'll die. I'll lose you again when I'm just getting used to the idea of having you with me forever."

I slide closer. "Forever sounds good."

"It does, but this job could steal you away."

"You're the one who was nearly killed by JJ's asshole friend months ago," I say, caressing her healed bottom lip.

Ruby frowns, having never considered her experience a near-death one. She tends to allow personal pain to roll off her back while her loved ones' suffering clings to her.

"I'll be careful by being smart," I tell Ruby as my arms slide around her shoulders. "I'll think things through before I do them. I'll keep my ego in check. When I'm not sure how to handle something, I'll ask for help. I'll never forget it's a job, not who I am."

"You sound so certain."

142

"That's how I feel, but I need you to help me. The talk with you before meeting Cooper helped settle my nerves. I don't have anyone else I can trust like that. Everyone else thinks of me as the stripper or Howler's son or the twins' buddy. They see me as soft. I need you to see me as more. Or else I can't see myself that way."

Ruby studies me again, but her eyes no longer hold fear and anger. "You're still my Bonn. Older and wiser, but you're still the boy I fell in love with, right?"

"Yep, and you're still my Ruby. That's why we can't share a room without becoming magnets."

Crawling into my lap, Ruby rests her head on my shoulder. "I want to dream, but I'm scared to want too much and end up with nothing."

"I'm afraid of not dreaming at all and losing everything."

Ruby nods before falling silent against me. I hold her for a long time as we think about the uncertain paths before us. We never guessed our lives would end up where we are now, leaving us unable to know what awaits us tomorrow.

FORTY - BONN

Entering Hayes's office building with Chevelle and Ruby, I find him leaning against a desk. He doesn't so much as glance at me, and I get the impression he's engaged in a staring contest with Candy's son. The boy stares at the much larger man, and they refuse to stop, even knowing they have company.

"Chevelle," I announce, "these are Hayes's kids."

Candy pokes her head out from behind Hayes and looks us over.

"You brought a distraction," she says, walking between her son and Hayes. "Good thinking, strip…"

An inhuman warning noise erupts from my throat. My pissed growl draws the attention of Hayes and a smile from Candy.

"Shame is such a waste of time," Candy teases me before focusing on Chevelle. "Would you like to play outside with Cricket and Chipper while the grownups talk about boring stuff?"

Chevelle nods but doesn't move even after the twins—a brunette girl and a blond boy—walk to the back door. They stare at her, and she stares back. Another staring contest ensues until Ruby takes Chevelle's hand and joins her outside.

"She's shy," I tell Candy.

"So am I."

"No doubt."

"Stop talking to her," Hayes grumbles and gives me a head nod to say he wants to speak alone.

"He's insecure," Candy whispers, giving me a wink.

"You're trying to get me killed."

"Well, you did make that weird noise to shut me up."

Following Hayes, I shoot Candy a dirty look, leading to her laughter. Once in the office, I shut the door and sit across from the grumpy giant.

"What the fuck is with you?" Hayes asks.

144

"I think not getting laid for a long time broke something in me."

"Yeah, that'll do it. Now that I've spent five million dollars, what's the next part of your big fucking plan?"

"I explain to the local dealers and hookers how you're their new boss. Make sure they know to stop skimming off the top unless they want to die."

"You aren't scary. What if they laugh in your face?"

"I break something on one of them. If that doesn't work, I'll break more shit until they get the message."

"You like beating on people?"

"No, but I've done worse to make money."

"Stripping for housewives can't be all that bad."

"You underestimate their grabby hands."

Hayes grins. "I don't want this fucked up."

"Sounds about right. I figure I'll need an office in Common Bend. Something close to the trailer parks where most of the business is run. I need to be seen often, so they feel our presence like they haven't with the Reapers. I want them to constantly look over their shoulders and think we're watching. That's the only way their type will obey."

"Fear is a good fucking motivator. I don't want to waste time and money coddling those fuckers. If they steal from me, I know people who can replace them," Hayes says and then adds, "And that goes for you. While this might be your fucking idea, I didn't know you existed until a week ago. You don't mean shit to me right now."

"Fair enough, but I want to build in Common Bend what you have in White Horse. The illegal shit will become so efficient it'll be invisible to outside eyes."

"You're good with words, and you talked Johansson into bending over. I still want my guy to work with you until your big plans are more than fucking promises. Moot runs the dirty shit in White Horse, and he has my ear. If you convince him, you'll convince me. I have no fucking interest in holding your hand during this process."

"Have him meet me at the old pesticide factory tomorrow at noon. I'll get the word out to the dealers and pimps. We'll have things rolling before summer."

Hayes leans back in his chair, making it groan under him. He plays with an unlit cigar and stares at the wall.

"Camden asked me for help awhile back. He wanted his wife to get a job at a local school. In exchange, he made clear he'd owe me. With him taking over the Brotherhood, that favor does me some good. Except he isn't running shit yet. Any idea when your old man and Camden's shitbag father will get the fuck out of the way so the pretty boy twins can take over?"

"No, but I can find out."

"And you'd sell them out for me?"

"You're paying my salary, and they're not. Besides, your interests and theirs intersect. Mojo and Howler stand in everyone's way."

"I like the way you say your old man's name. I hear a hint of rage in it. That's good because you're about to piss off a lot of fucking people in Hickory Creek."

"They were never going to rule Common Bend, and it's time they came to terms with that reality."

"Your father kills his enemies, and you're making yourself a big fucking target."

"Well, that's a funny thing because I plan to tell people how I represent your interests. You know, so if they fuck with me, they're fucking with you."

Hayes smirks. "Using me as your attack dog, huh? Nice, but don't think I'll clean up your messes."

"I don't plan to make any."

"You talk a good game. But if you weren't Howler's kid and tight with the twins, I don't see me letting you through the front door."

"I hear a lot of uncertainty in you. Are you backing out of the deal?"

Hayes narrows his dark eyes and gives me one hell of a "fuck you" look. I've challenged his ego, and nothing pisses off a guy like him more than implying he doesn't behave like a top dog.

"Let's get something straight," he says with his jaw tight and eyes still glaring. "You do right by me, and I'll do right by you. If you fuck up, I won't care that your kid is playing with mine. I'll just end you and send Ruby a check for her pain and suffering. We understand each other?"

"Yes, but you need to understand that I've quit my stripping and construction jobs. I have no money coming in to support my family, so let's get this thing moving along," I casually say since I expected Hayes to threaten me. "Besides, we don't want the twats in Common Bend having time to plot shit. The faster we move in, the fewer people we'll need to kill to get them under control."

Hayes stares at me for maybe a minute before nodding. "Let's talk numbers and logistics."

For the next twenty minutes, Hayes and I discuss weapons, money, and muscle. I plan to meet with the sheriff to ensure he knows who calls the shots in Common Bend now. Hayes no longer gives me his pissed asshole look by the time we walk out of the office. With his backing, I'm more than ready to start knocking heads together in Common Bend.

FORTY ONE - RUBY

Candy promises Elle will be fine in the yard behind the office. I'm less worried about the location than the company my daughter is keeping. Candy's son and daughter are the same age as Elle, but they're twins and weird and really into showing people how bizarre they can be. In fact, the girl warned me of their growing psychic powers. When I only stared at her, she and the boy shared an approving nod.

"They like to screw with people," Candy proudly announces after the twins leave me frowning.

Now, the three kids are in the backyard, kicking a ball and talking about summer break.

"Even with homeschooling, they treat vacations as a huge load off their little shoulders," Candy says, taking her seat behind her desk. "If you want something to drink, there's a kitchen over there. I'd serve you, but I'm on a break."

I lean against the wall and watch the kids play. My mind is on Bonn starting his enforcer job for Hayes. Despite his reassurances, I'm stuck on the fear that I'll lose him again, and this time forever.

"Can I ask you something?"

Candy looks up from her phone for long enough to shrug. "Have at it."

"Do you worry someone Hayes crosses will walk up one day and end him?"

"Nope."

Though her answer doesn't shock me, I'm still disappointed to hear it. "Because you think he's indestructible?"

"I wish he was, but that's not it. See, I figure life will go one of two ways. Say someone does end him, well, then I'll be in a world of pain that no amount of worrying ahead of time will prepare me for. Why suffer in preparation for suffering? The other option is no one ends Hayes, and I've spent years worrying over nothing. Either way, I'd stress myself out for no benefit."

Nodding, I realize how much sense her words make. I have an easy choice. Whether I worry or not, I can't change what happens in the future. Besides, even if Bonn quits the job and works a boring nine-to-five career, I could still lose him.

"I never thought Bonn would be involved in this kind of life," I say because I think it and not because I sense Candy wants to talk. "He never showed any interest in the Brotherhood."

"Bikers smell," Candy mutters. "My sister loves one, and I tell her that he smells. She tells me that she likes that he smells. Her old husband was an abusive ass, so I guess she has low standards."

"My sister is married to a biker."

"Does he smell?"

"Don't all men smell?"

"Possibly, but I haven't smelled them all."

Smiling, I shake my head. "Do you like having a son?"

"Yes. Chipper is easier to deal with than Cricket. He's mellow. Like when he plots, I can't sense him doing it, and I prefer to be surprised."

"Can I ask how you came up with their names?"

"Their dad chose them to punish me. What he didn't realize was how much I enjoy punishing other people. Forcing average folks to say my kids' names is quite entertaining. What about Chevelle?"

"I looked on baby name sites for something Jamaican to honor my father's side of the family. That one stood out. I also liked how I could give her a nickname, which seemed important since I couldn't have one with my name."

"Didn't want to go by 'Rub,' huh? Or would it be 'Rube'?"

"Either way, I wasn't a fan."

Outside, the kids sit on the ground now. Cricket has her arm around Elle as if they're plotting something devious. My daughter is custom-made to become someone's minion, and I've unknowingly introduced her to two evil masterminds.

"They're harmless," Candy says, having read my mind. "For now, anyway. I don't envy the people who think life will be easier when Hayes retires one day. Instead of one asshole, they'll deal with two."

When I frown at her, Candy looks up from her phone and shrugs. "I might be named Candy, but I don't sugarcoat things, and those two are assholes to people they don't like. Fortunately, they love their mama."

Her proud smile eases my frown. "I probably worry too much."

"Probably. It's a woman's way to second guess, overthink, and worry shit to death."

"Can you blame us when we're the ones left to clean up the mess?"

"I'd rather fearlessly make a mess than sit around worrying about how bad it'll be, but that's just me."

Did Candy just call me a wuss? I don't know her well enough to be offended. She's also not paying enough attention to the conversation for me to be certain she made a personal dig. While our men work together now and our kids become quick pals, Candy and I likely won't be sharing a girls' night out anytime soon.

FORTY TWO - BONN

Unlike a lot of girls her age, Chevelle lacks the urge to grow up immediately. She doesn't want to wear makeup or try out heels. She's never asked for a phone of her own, knowing she spends all her time at school where she can't use one or with her family who will let her borrow theirs. Even when she dances, her movements are childlike. Lots of jumping up and down rather than attempting to move her hips like the preteens I saw earlier in the day.

My baby plans to stay a baby and considers three-year-old Keanu to be her best friend. The boy is also jumping up and down in our trailer, making noises to go along with Chevelle's karaoke singing of "Walk Like an Egyptian."

Ruby bobs her head to the music while working on a big pot of Hamburger Helper. I stand halfway between my singing daughter and my humming woman, unsure what I should do with myself. I don't know if I've gotten bigger or the trailers are smaller, but I feel claustrophobic here.

"Are you staying tonight?" Ruby whispers, suddenly next to me.

I shiver at her warm breath against my jaw. Her deep brown eyes steal my unease until I'm smiling like a fool.

"Can I?"

"Is that a real question?"

Nodding, I caress her cheek with my knuckles. Her skin is so soft, and her gaze so tender that I'd never leave her side.

"I like having you around," she says, stepping away and making me work for a kiss.

I nearly tackle Ruby before pressing my lips to hers. Laughing, she glances at Chevelle, who smiles at us.

"Your mom is so pretty," I tell Chevelle while hugging Ruby tighter.

Covering her mouth, Chevelle giggles. "She is pretty."

"So, should I keep her?"

Nodding, Chevelle sets down the microphone and shuffles toward us nervously. I reach out for her, and our girl immediately melts into the hug. Ruby wraps us tighter, embracing the idea of us. We're making a go at building a family again. This time, I refuse to fail.

FORTY THREE - BONN

Salty Peanuts has been passed down in the Hallstead family for generations. I don't know who originally built the bar or if it was a rough place before the Brotherhood took control. No matter the history, the twins enjoy a cold beer there a few nights a week.

Tonight, they've invited me to have a drink. I find Dayton at a back table when I arrive. He's already bleary-eyed from starting his drinking hours earlier.

"Why are we here?" Dayton asks when I sit down.

"I thought Camden wanted to bond with a couple of men after spending so much time around Daisy."

"You'd think, but nope. The asshole has no time for anyone except his woman."

Ignoring the glare on Dayton's face, I watch the door until Camden arrives. He joins us and makes small talk about the Hallstead sisters buying De Campo's. He claims Mojo won't shut up about the missed opportunity of opening the town's fourth strip club where the restaurant stands.

"They live in the past," Dayton mumbles. "Mojo has a hard-on about the strip club like Howler does with Common Bend."

Camden snaps his fingers and points at his brother. "Common Bend is in play. Word is the Reapers are pulling up their stakes and leaving Tennessee."

"Only because Hayes bought Common Bend," I say, figuring I ought to shut down any big plans they might have brewing.

The twins give me matching frowns, making me wonder if I'd jumped the truth gun.

Dayton leans forward and growls, "How the fuck would you know that?"

"Wait, where did you go with Ruby and Chevelle again?" Camden asks in a calmer tone.

"I negotiated the deal for Hayes, so my trip was to Kentucky."

"Why the fuck would you do that?" Dayton asks.

"I saw an opportunity to better my stock and took it. Like you said, I can't strip forever."

"Hayes came to you?" Camden asks, but he knows the answer. "Is this about Howler?"

"Screwing him over is only one of the perks."

"What about screwing us over?" Dayton demands, pounding on the table hard enough to knock over his beer. "Shit."

"Calm down," Camden warns him.

"Shut the fuck up."

"You need to find the cooldown button in your fat head and keep pushing it until you remember how the fuck old you are."

"You don't get shit."

Camden rolls his eyes and then focuses on me. "You kinda screwed us here, you know?"

"How so? You didn't want Common Bend. Now, your father can't waste time with a pissing contest between the Brotherhood and Reapers."

"Hayes expanding his power ain't helpful, though."

"He feels the same about the Brotherhood."

"So, you took his side?" Dayton asks, taking the new beer the waitress brings.

When she tries to clean up the mess, he grabs the towel and waves her away. I watch him drop the cloth on the floor and use his foot to move it around until the beer is mostly soaked up. Dayton never looks away from me while he does his half-ass cleaning job.

"You are making enemies," he says.

"Are you threatening me?"

"Me? No, I'm a fucking softie, but the Brotherhood doesn't get their marching orders from Cam and me, do they?"

"Are you worried Howler will kill me?"

"Why not? It's not like he doesn't have plenty of backup sons to take your place."

"I guess I'll need to deal with him, then."

"Oh, boy, look who's playing the tough guy now."

154

"Dayton, stop," Camden says, sighing heavily. "Maybe this thing can work for us."

"Who the fuck is us?"

"You and me, dummy." Before Dayton can speak, Camden turns to me. "You're working for Hayes now?"

"Yeah. I'll supervise Common Bend for him."

"Good luck with that, asshole," Dayton grumbles, standing up and walking away.

I glance back at where he sits at the bar, watching the TV.

"Ignore him," Camden says.

"Why is he such a bitch lately?"

"He's dealing with something, but don't ask me what. I see him running around with that asshole JJ, even though he ought to hate the guy. Dayton is a mystery most days."

"I know you want to expand club territory south. If I thought you wanted Common Bend once you're president, I wouldn't have made my move."

Camden nods. "This can work out for everyone. Well, not our dads, but they had their moments in the fucking sun. Let them pout now. With you in control of Common Bend, I don't have to worry about the Reapers on my north border. Hayes has no interest in Hickory Creek, does he?"

"Not that I can tell. His main concern is keeping White Horse gentrified."

"So, you and Hayes buffer the Reapers up north and east. That keeps the club's eyes directed south. Nashville is where we'll increase our money and power. Mojo and Howler won't like it, but their time is limited."

"How limited?"

Camden curls his upper lip and gives me a dark frown. "I won't grow old waiting for them to retire."

Nodding, I glance at Dayton at the bar top. "I didn't want to lie to you guys, but you'd have to tell Mojo once you knew. I couldn't ask you to be disloyal to your club, even if we're family."

"Yeah, I get it. Daisy's been complaining about how Ruby keeps shit secret. I'm sure she'll be happy to have things out in the open."

"Should I worry about Howler making an example of me?"

"Howler? No, probably not. His sisters are pissed about De Campo's burning down. They think JJ did it, and they're looking for a reason to get rid of him. So, I can't see them taking kindly to Howler protecting his shit son and punishing the one they like."

"I don't know that they like me."

"They asked Ruby to work at De Campo's. They show off Chevelle in family pictures. Yeah, you're in their good graces. Not always easy to tell with them, of course, but I know the signs."

"Good to hear."

"Also, they benefit from Common Bend quieting down. If you and Hayes give them that, they'll like you even more. The Hallstead sisters are about the bottom line. They put up with the club's wild ways, but they have no patience for trouble spilling over from Common Bend."

"We're good, then?"

"You and me? Sure. Dayton has a huge crush on you, so don't let him tell you otherwise."

We glance back at where his brother rests his head on the bar top.

"He drinks too much," I say.

"Always."

"No, somehow, he's managed to outdo himself lately."

"Should we schedule an intervention?"

"Who would come to that? The Hallstead sisters believe in allowing people to crush themselves under the weight of their failures. The club thinks alcohol is the great equalizer." When I frown at his wording, Camden smiles. "Everyone is stupid and weak when drunk. Get it?"

"Yeah."

"I guess we could get the girls to come. Harmony could tell him how she overcame her obsession with aliens or whatever it was that she used to obsess over."

"Cryptids is what she obsesses over. You know, like the Loch Ness Monster and Bigfoot."

"Much better."

156

"I don't think he cares what she says as long as she's wearing something low-cut when she says it."

Smiling, Camden shifts in his chair as if finished talking about Dayton. "Do you have the muscle to help you break the assholes in Common Bend?"

"Hayes has guys. One of them is hooked up with his sister-in-law. At least, that's what Candy told me for no reason."

"Yeah, that's Moot. The only reason he never hooked up with the Brotherhood was that he's loyal to Hayes. If you need help, you let me know."

"Hayes won't like having the club involved in Common Bend."

"I didn't say anything about the club. I was talking about if you needed my help as your cousin and good friend. Sure, I don't nurse a fucking crush on you like Dayton, but I want to see you succeed. Get your woman and kid back and live a good life. All the happy shit I've got for myself."

"Aren't you a peach?" I say, smirking.

"The best of the bunch. That's what my mom says, anyway."

"Yeah, and she'd never say that to your brothers."

"Of course not. The woman is a saint and has never lied in her entire life."

"Must be nice. I feel like all I do lately is lie."

"There are times when you got to bullshit people to make big moves. You've been sitting on the sidelines for too long. Now, you're doing shit, and that's the right idea. The way you're winning back Ruby is a good thing, too. I'm surprised it took you so long."

"I was worried I'd try and fail."

"What changed your mind?"

"Watching you crash and burn with Daisy but still end up with the girl in the end."

"I'm a fucking inspiration. If that ain't the truth."

"So, we're really good?"

"No deception. I've been thinking a lot about the future, and this news makes my plans easier."

"Well, that's all that really matters."

157

"Now, you need to tell Ruby to open up to Daisy, and I'll be a happy man. When the sisters don't share every fart, they get tense, and I can't deal with an unhappy Daisy."

"I'll get on that."

"Good deal."

Camden babbles a bit about Daisy's cats, but his mind is on Dayton, Common Bend, and the future. No doubt, he'll have more questions for me. Tonight, he's lost in his head.

I know the feeling.

With the truth out, I'm short on time to get Common Bend under control. If the place flounders, Hayes will look weak, and the Brotherhood's current management might get ideas about taking what Howler's wanted for decades.

FORTY FOUR - RUBY

The new restaurant's outer walls are up. On the inside, plumbers and electricians climb over each other to ensure work gets done on schedule. The Hallstead women have little sympathy for delays. Piss them off, and suddenly work permits get yanked, licenses revoked, and the IRS wants to audit.

Across the street, we meet with Clara, Eloise, and De Campo's old chef. Sally is half-asleep from working double shifts at her current job before coming home to brainstorm with me for a few hours on the proposed menu. We didn't finish until after midnight, so Mom is lucky she isn't drooling on herself.

I hand the women and Chef Aaron copies of the menus I made at the UPS store that morning.

"This isn't what I imagined," Aaron says in a snooty tone.

Sally stops yawning long enough to mumble, "Hickory Creek already has a decent Italian restaurant. What all the Italian places in this area have in common is they're geared for adults."

"To compete in a saturated market," I continue, "we should be a family restaurant where parents can come with little ones without worrying about making noise or a mess."

"I like it," Clara announces. "The Brotherhood wanted to stick a strip club here, but we'll build a family restaurant instead. Yes, I like that a lot."

Sally gives me a side glance filled with uncertainty. With the Hallstead women remain so focused on pissing off the Brotherhood, we can't help wondering what happens when they eventually make peace with Mojo and Howler? Will this restaurant be tossed aside and us with it?

"I don't cook for children," Aaron mutters.

"Listen," I say, losing my patience with his pissy little frown. "If you can't handle making good food for little people, you need to find another job. Or maybe you could

159

think of this as a challenge. Can you make a veggie lasagna good enough for a kid to eat? Can you manage tiny breadsticks? Just think outside the box, okay?"

Clara and Eloise turn their amused gazes to Aaron, who shows no reaction.

"I'll see what I can do," he finally mumbles, clearly remembering who signs his checks.

"I'm sure you will," Eloise says coolly. "We want to create a Hickory Creek staple, not just any old dive."

"We can name the new place La Famiglia," Clara says, smirking. "It'll be entertaining to force Howler to mangle the name every time he complains."

I peek at Sally to find her struggling to keep her eyes open. She's so tired I doubt she's worried about anything besides climbing into bed for a few hours.

I finish up with the sisters and Aaron as quickly as possible, so I can drive my mom home. She shuffles off to her trailer, mumbling about mini-meatballs and ravioli.

I head into my place and pile dirty clothes into a basket to take to Bonn's condo. I do love his laundry room but not enough to leave Lush Gardens.

While waiting for the load to finish, I mop the floor and vacuum and many other pointless activities in the already clean condo. No doubt, I fear if I sit down on the comfy couch and watch TV on the big screen that I might reconsider my current living arrangements. Even the view out the third-story condo lures me into dreaming bigger than I should. *Who wouldn't want to wake up every morning to the sight of a geese-filled pond?*

By the time I return to my trailer, I'm desperate for a distraction, but Elle will be at school for another hour.

Folding clothes, I smile at how long it's been since I washed one of Bonn's shirts. I recall how he'd done work on Mom's trailer, getting filthy in the process. I'd taken his shirt to wash while he walked around bare-chested. I couldn't get enough of that view.

Today, I admire the fabric on his black T-shirt and think about how it slides over his wide shoulders and down his hard chest. Eventually, I stop molesting the shirt long enough to exchange it for mine. Standing in front of the mirror, I ignore my silly smile and instead think about how much I love having Bonn back in my life.

Reality startles me away from the mirror when I hear Harmony arriving home early. I peek out the shades to find her fumbling with her keys. Even from across the walkway, I can see she's been crying.

When I hurry outside to help her, she thanks me through her sobs.

"What happened?" I ask, walking inside with her.

Her voice cracking and tears spilling down her already red-stained face, Harmony says, "Anita died."

"How?" I ask, hugging her to me.

"She was taking her afternoon nap on the living room couch. I checked on her every fifteen minutes. During one check, she was sleeping. During the next, she was gone. I tried to revive her, but it was too late."

Harmony worked as Anita Hall's health care aide for nearly two years. I know she loved the disabled old woman like family. My sister's always been a sensitive soul, and I often worried about her reaction to this inevitable painful day.

Later that afternoon, Bonn takes Elle and Keanu to McDonald's, so I can console Harmony. Soon, Daisy arrives, and Mom orders pizza. In the kitchen, Betty makes mojitos, but no matter what we say and do, Harmony only stares at the wall.

I brush her blonde hair and tell her everything will be okay. How she took such good care of Anita, who is now safe in Heaven. I say all the normal stuff, except Harmony heard these words years ago when Keanu's father died.

Mojitos, pizza, and cheap uplifting words won't ease her pain. Only a smiling Keanu excited about his Happy Meal toy perks up Harmony. Focusing on her son reminds her of the present when her mind would rather suffer with the past.

FORTY FIVE - BONN

Moot shows up twenty minutes late to the abandoned factory, leaving me tense from too much time planning shit that hasn't happened. A tall, kinda scrawny guy, he runs his hand through messy, blond hair and rubs his bleary eyes. Thinking he's hungover, I'm instantly pissed.

Moot gives me a sleepy smile. "I got a cold running through my house. Kids were up all night, coughing and rubbing snot everywhere."

Nodding, I force my tense shoulders to relax. "Are you ready?"

"All business, aren't ya?"

"Hayes isn't paying me to look pretty."

"Don't go spoiling him with your work ethic and make the rest of us look bad," Moot says, running both hands through his hair in the hopes of corralling a serious case of bedhead.

"I want to get this over with, so I can start looking for a house."

"Why would you want to move to Common Bend?" he asks, following me down the broken concrete path to a long-abandoned factory door.

"This is where I work, so I figure it's where I'll live. Besides, I can't stay in Hickory Creek much longer."

"Naw, I bet the Brotherhood ain't happy to have you around."

Pausing before opening the door, I exhale slowly. To my right, Moot wraps a blue bandana over his messy hair.

"How come you never worked for the Brotherhood?" I ask him.

"They were too high class for my taste."

I can't tell if he's kidding or not, but I guess it doesn't matter. Once his hair is properly hidden, I open the door and walk inside to where two dozen people wait.

These dealers and top prostitutes in Common Bend are now my problems. Employees, in a way, they'll make or break my reign as Hayes's henchman.

I scan their faces while Moot makes a beeline for a particular meth dealer. He punches the twitchy asshole in the stomach. A few women gasp, but the rest of the people put on their best professional faces. Moot drags the guy to me.

Having never been a violent man, I lost most fights in my life. I've always lacked the blood lust to hurt my opponents in the way they needed hurting. *Today will be different.*

Rather than hate this piece of shit standing before me, I focus on how he's an obstacle to my family's happiness. Much like how I thought about Ruby and Chevelle when stripping so I could ignore the seedier elements of my job, I now think of them while punching the dealer in the jaw.

He falls to the ground, spitting up blood and cursing my mother. I kick him in the ribs and then land my foot hard against his scrawny left leg. The bone cracks under the pressure, startling a man nearby.

"Angus Hayes now owns Common Bend," I announce, using my foot on his cheek to keep the dealer from moving. "He expects me to run the day-to-day. I guess that makes me your boss."

"Is this your way of making us like you?" asks a dark-haired prostitute.

"Cheeze here skimmed from the profits before sending them to the Reapers. All of you have skimmed," I say, scanning their faces. "That's the past. You stole from the Reapers, but you won't steal from Hayes. If you do, you will receive one warning like Cheeze is now. After that, you'll be replaced."

I dig the heel of my boot into the meth dealer's ribs, making him cry out.

"Hayes is a businessman," I continue. "He expects you to behave like business people. You have merchandise that costs you a certain amount and sells for a certain amount. Those numbers better make sense to a businessman like Hayes. If you think you can cheat him, you will be replaced.

If you do your job, you will make money, he will make money, and the law will stay out of the way."

Cheeze slaps my leg, wanting me to get off him. I move my foot from his chest to his throat and give him a warning nudge. He immediately quiets down.

"We are all replaceable. Every single one of us. Don't ever think you're special. You are a cog in the machine. If you do your job, the machine is happy. If you misfire, the machine will replace you with a new part."

Scanning their faces again, I continue, "Finally, I know you have spent the last year with several different bosses. The various sheriffs have run from friendly to hostile to the current weakling. You've got it in your head that you can do whatever you want if you keep your head down. You think you can take more clients than you claim and steal the money. That worked fine with your former bosses, but Hayes has eyes everywhere. Your clients, your neighbors, your kids' teachers, anyone could snitch you out. If you do wrong by Hayes, there'll be nowhere to hide. Simple as that."

I take my foot off Cheeze's throat and extend a hand to help him up.

"As far as I'm concerned, you're all on my shitlist," I say, looking for troublemakers. "I know you've stolen from the Reapers, and you'll no doubt try to do the same with Hayes. I expect you to test me. The smarter ones won't need a beating to learn, but I still plan to break each one of you. Now, I suggest you go home and think long and hard about how you've run your businesses and whether you want to continue working in Common Bend."

When I gesture for Moot to follow me, he does so while yawning widely.

"Nice speech. Are you sure you don't want to kill anyone to make a point?"

"Not yet. Give them a few days to mull over their options. The first one to test us will suffer a messy death. That ought to get the rest of the holdouts in order."

"Hayes didn't say anything about muscle in Common Bend. Are you planning to use the cops or bring in your guys?"

"I know a few large fuckers who could use the work. They got on the wrong side of the Brotherhood, which works in our benefit. We don't want the club thinking they have friendly faces in Common Bend."

"What about the cops?"

"What about them?" I ask as we now stand next to my SUV.

"They think they run this place for the Reapers. Are you planning on telling them different?"

"I'll have a quick conversation with the sheriff, but there's no need to make a big deal out of it. They weren't running shit when they claimed to be calling the shots. If they were, I wouldn't be here now."

Moot scratches his covered head. "Hayes wants me to stay close to you until you're set up. He isn't sure your balls are big enough for the job."

"Good. I'd worry if he trusted me so easily."

"Dude, he barely trusts me, and I went to prison to protect his business. The guy has issues."

"Wouldn't be where he is if he didn't," I say, giving Moot a smile. "Thanks for the help this morning, but maybe you better get some rest."

Nodding, Moot yawns again before heading home. I think about how Hayes called the guy a workhorse. Moot offers no flash, only results. I'd be glad if everyone I worked with was as competent. Since I suspect they won't be, I'll need to spill blood again.

I'm not a violent man, but I will cross nearly any line to make a good life for my family. After today, I'm one step closer.

FORTY SIX - RUBY

Bonn stands at the pond, wearing a shit-eating grin that pisses me off. He's turning into Hayes, and I didn't sign on for that crap. I need my sweet-as-sin Bonn.

Well, this isn't entirely true. My sweet boy buckled under the pressure of becoming a father. The new Bonn knows what he wants and defends his family. While I appreciate his newfound focus, his big dog arrogance rubs me in the wrong way.

"I know it doesn't matter now. Yet, I wanted to come clean, so you'd know and wouldn't think I was hiding anything," I say, hoping to start trouble.

Bonn glances down at me, smiles confidently, and makes me want to slap him. He's got everything he wants now. Bonn sees the past as insignificant and figures I ought to forgive and forgot.

"I had a one-night stand years ago," I lie.

Bonn immediately shakes his head. "No, you didn't."

I'm instantly angered by his complete certainty that I'd never find a single other dick to ride in the entire world. *No way am I telling the truth now!*

"It was at a party, and he was from out of town. Just a quickie and not good enough for me to mention to anyone. So, we're not so different. You had Kim. I had this guy."

"You're lying."

"No, I'm not," I growl, hating his stupid, arrogant expression.

"What's his name?"

"I don't remember. I think it started with an 'S,' but who knows?"

"You're full of crap," he says, suddenly standing too close.

"Stop crowding me."

"Tell me his name."

"I told you that I don't know."

"You had sex with a guy whose name you didn't know."

"I'd been drinking."

"What did he look like?"

"What does it matter?"

"Tell me."

"Why?"

"I want to find him."

"What for?" I ask, walking away.

Bonn instantly follows me, remaining too close for comfort. "I want to see the man who knows your body."

"Why?"

"I need to hurt him."

"Can I hurt Kim for knowing your body?"

"Sure. Now, who's this guy? I don't believe you don't remember. You never drink enough to forget things like that."

"I did that night," I mutter, refusing to fess up now.

"No."

"Stop following me."

"Tell me."

"Stop bugging me."

"Ruby, tell me now," he demands and uses my shirt to tug me to a stop.

"Back off," I say, grabbing a handful of dirt off the ground. "I'm not kidding."

"Go ahead and throw it. I'm still finding out."

Overwhelmed by how my ruse backfired, I realize I need to end this now. "There's nothing to find out."

"Tell me."

"Stop saying that."

"Tell me."

"Ugh. I'm going inside."

When I walk away, Bonn grabs my shirt and holds me still. "Tell me."

"I was lying, okay? There was no one else."

"Tell me."

"I just did."

"So, you were lying then or now? How can I know which?"

Glaring up at him, I mutter, "I'm not taking a lie detector if that's what you're suggesting."

"Tell me."

"Stop saying that!"

Bonn gives me a mournful sigh before sweeping me over his shoulder. "We need to figure this thing out."

"You're an idiot."

"You started this by mentioning another man."

"I'm so very sorry. I only wanted to mess with you. I mean, you got to have sex with someone besides me. Now, let me down."

Bonn says nothing. He just keeps walking like a soldier off to war. I think to fight him, but I really don't want to fall off his shoulder and land on the hard ground. *Why not let him have his stupid macho moment while I check out his ass flexing with every step?*

"Did I miss something?" Sally asks when Bonn stops at her trailer.

"Can you watch Chevelle tonight?" he asks while our daughter walks around to see me hanging from him.

"Are you okay?" she asks, weirded out.

"Your father is a nerd."

Elle smiles at me. "Are you in trouble?"

"No."

"Yes," Bonn corrects. "But you know I don't spank, so she'll be fine."

Elle finds his comment hilarious, making me wonder what she'd think if he did spank. My kid laughs behind her hand and then runs away to likely snitch me out to Harmony.

Mom bends down to look me in the eye. "This is good?"

"Despite my current position, I actually have the upper hand here."

Smiling, she gestures for Bonn to keep going. He obeys and marches to my trailer. I know he's taking me to bed, where he thinks he can bully me into admitting what I already did. *Bonn really is a nerd.*

Bonn dumps me on my bed and walks to the closet. I watch him while considering if making a run for it is worth the effort.

"Sometimes, a man can't control himself," Bonn says, climbing on the bed where I rest my head on a pillow.

"What is that?" I ask, seeing something hanging from his left hand.

"I own exactly two ties. You're looking at them."

Before I realize what he's doing, Bonn straddles me, pinning my body to the bed. He takes one of my wrists and wraps a tie around it. I struggle to get free, but he easily binds me to the bed. Though I fight him with the second wrist, Bonn only smiles.

"You're making my dick hard."

I look at his crotch a few inches from my face. His bulge is clear, and I imagine that massive cock spending some quality time between my legs.

Bonn climbs off me once I'm bound to the bed. I watch him strip out of his clothes and stand before me with a thick, menacing erection.

"I need to fuck the truth out of you. I won't lie that it might take a while, and you might beg me to stop, but there's no other way."

"Have you lost your mind?" I ask, yanking at the binds. "If you wanted to play in bed, you could have just asked."

"This isn't a game. I want you to tell me everything about that guy or prove to me that you were lying."

"How would I do that?"

"I guess we'll find out."

Sighing, I plan to give him a speech to end all speeches about how he's an idiot who ought to thank his lucky stars anyone puts up with his shit. Before I can unleash my temper on him, he yanks up my shirt and bra with one violent move. I flinch at his aggression and even consider using my knee to end his good time.

Then, my tit begs me to keep my fat mouth shut as Bonn latches on and sucks roughly. He isn't playing, but my nipples still think he's the best guy ever.

"Bonn," I mumble, somewhere between irritated and appreciative.

"I need to know," he growls, holding my nipple between his teeth.

"I wish I could help you, but I don't know how."

My initial plan of getting him to untie me and fuck off has now been replaced by the strategy of having him fuck me a bit and then doing that other stuff. After all, I've been inconvenienced by his behavior, so I might as well enjoy a little pleasure.

Bonn runs his tongue flat against one tit, bathing it in saliva before sliding it across my chest to my neglected nipple. I smile at the pleasure, totally oblivious to the way his cock angrily pokes at my bare thigh. Even knowing he wants to fuck, I'm unconcerned about the details.

Lifting my hips, Bonn holds me up with one hand while tugging off my shorts and underwear. He tosses them aside before spreading my legs wide.

"Your pussy will tell me the truth," he says, staring at the flesh he spreads with his fingers.

"Sure."

Bonn bends forward and gives my pussy a deep lick. Moaning immediately, I tug at the binds without thinking.

"You won't get loose until I'm certain what the truth is."

"Don't trust my pussy. She lies," I murmur, lifting my ass off the bed to give him a mouthful.

Bonn latches onto the flesh and sucks hungrily until my knees buckle. Soon, he takes my left leg and presses it toward my stomach before leaning into me and shoving the head of his cock in the flesh still abuzz over his tongue. He thrusts three or four times before pulling out and wiping his wet dick against my thigh.

"This guy didn't have a name, but what did he look like?"

"There was no other guy," I whisper, watching him rub the head of his cock against my clit. "Bonn, I'm close."

"I'll let you come once, but then you and I need to find the truth."

Before I can respond, he leans down and shoves his hands under my ass to lift me up. His mouth finds a perfect angle over my clit. Feasting on my swollen nub, Bonn sends me into a fit of pleasure before I can even catch my breath. I somehow whimper "no" while begging him for more. My entire body flushes with sweat, and I roll my hips against his wet face.

"Tell me what he looked like," Bonn demands, resting me back on the bed and driving his cock into me.

"I don't remember," I babble, now that my brain is no longer running the show. "Bonn, fuck me."

Instantly, he pulls out his cock and shows me the angry red head. "Your pussy wants me to believe you," he says, slapping his dick against my clit. "I don't know, though."

Bonn shoves inside me again. He props himself over my body and fucks me hard until his face tenses. Pulling out his cock, he shoots his thick cum on my left thigh and then the right. Once every drop leaves him, Bonn caresses the jizz into my legs and over my pussy.

"You were always such a good liar," he says, but I don't know if he's talking to me or my pussy.

"There was no one else," I whisper.

Bonn stands effortlessly on the lumpy bed and steps over me before lowering himself until his cock slides against my lips.

"Suck my balls. Make me so hard I can fuck the truth out of you."

I wish I had an ounce of self-control, but my body refuses to tell this man no. I wet my lips and spread them around his balls. I watch him stroke his cock while I work at his perineum.

"I want to touch you," I say, nuzzling my cheek against his balls.

Bonn reaches over and unties one wrist. He takes my hand and wraps it around his cock.

"Make me harder," he demands.

My lips suck hungrily at his balls while my hand mercilessly pumps at his hard flesh. Minutes pass while I work him into another erection.

171

Bonn frees his cock from my grip and angles the head into my mouth. Sucking him, I want to taste the explosion of heat I know he's holding back. Before I can, Bonn tugs free his cock. I lick my lips after he caresses them with his leaking dick.

"You look so beautiful," he murmurs, moving on the bed until he's maneuvered my ass to the edge.

I reach over to untie my wrist, but Bonn gently slaps away my hand.

"Not yet. You haven't passed the truth test."

Before I can respond, Bonn shoves his cock into my pussy and fucks me roughly. Pumping his hips, he's close to coming after I sucked him off. The first time I gave him a blowjob, he came within a minute. When I asked if I could try again, I swear he almost cried.

Now, he punishes my pussy. I moan and use my free hand to caress my clit. Bonn covers my fingers with his and forces me to rub harder. I do what he wants and soon groan deep in my chest as the powerful orgasm sends me into a stupor.

Bonn doesn't come. Instead, he pulls out his cock and dips two fingers into my contracting pussy. He slathers my juices on my nipples, pinching each one for good measure.

"Oh, Bonn."

"I think your pussy is mad at you for lying to me."

I want to say something. Maybe I'll give him a piece of my mind, or perhaps I'll beg for another orgasm. I never speak, though, because my gaze focuses on Bonn bringing a fingertip of pre-cum to my left nipple. He does the same to my right one.

"These belong to me," he says, kneading my nipples into hard, angry points.

I only nod before he returns his cock to my pussy and fucks me again. I want him to come inside me, but he pulls out and unleashes on my stomach. Groaning my name, he strokes out everything his balls will provide.

I'm dying to untie my free hand but don't dare ask. Bonn's gaze is aggressive, and I wait to see what he wants now.

Kneeling, he shoves his tongue into my pussy and fucks the flesh in the way his cock just did. I wiggle and whine, fighting to reach another orgasm. He pushes away my fingers when they linger too close to my clit.

"Mine," he growls.

Nodding again, I bite back a squeal when he flicks my clit while nipping at my thigh.

Bonn startles me again by standing suddenly and reaching over to untie the bind. He flips me over before I can reach for him and shoves open my legs.

"Your ass is curvier than when we were kids," he says.

I don't know if he's praising or insulting me. His answer comes at the sting of his teeth on both cheeks. Sighing, I smile at the feel of him leaving hickeys on my backside.

Bonn's fingers tease my pussy and then my asshole. My body tenses and I wonder if he'll drive into my butt the way he did my pussy. We gave anal a try a few times as teenagers, but the pleasure and pain were too intense. I'd come so hard and cried so much that Bonn got scared of ever trying again.

Now, he teases my back door, and I wonder if I can endure what he's planning. My thoughts are on lubricant when he stands behind me and reaches over to tie my wrists together.

"Bonn, no," I complain without much effort.

"It soothes me to see you tied up. That way, you can't run away."

Again, my brain considers pointing out undeniable truths. And again, he kills my urge, to be honest.

Lifting my hips slightly, Bonn uses his thumb to tease my anus while his other hand makes my clit beg.

"Come for me," he whispers. "I want to eat your wet pussy."

My body quickly responds to the way he torments it. When he shoves his thumb into my anus, I cover my mouth to keep from screaming in pleasure. I close my eyes and fuck his hand wildly. He owns every inch of me. I swear if he told my body to jump, my pussy would instantly ask how high.

I don't even finish coming down from my orgasm before he kneels behind me and shoves his face into my pussy. While he laps up my juices, I hear his hand working his cock into a demanding erection.

Bonn keeps my legs spread while he maneuvers himself behind me. When I feel the head of his cock against my pussy, I wait for him to fill me. Bonn does so, but tenderly, slowly, almost cautiously. Smiling at his suddenly gentle touch, I glance back at him. He leans over to kiss me with his sticky lips.

"I need to fuck you until you can't stand," he whispers. "I need to fuck you until I believe you with every part of my soul. Even if I break my dick and rip apart your pussy, I can't stop."

For the last time, I attempt some semblance of logic. Bonn is moving so gingerly inside me. Though he can be reasoned with, my body betrays me. I can't get out a single word before a moan forms instead.

Bonn reaches under me, snatching a nipple and rolling it roughly in his fingers. He shoves his other hand between my legs, finds my clit, and makes it beg. As soon as I whimper his name approvingly, Bonn unleashes his powerful hips and fucks me until we're past caring about the truth.

FORTY SEVEN - BONN

Ruby collapses half on me after calling Chevelle to ensure she has everything for a night at her grandma's trailer. I reach across my chest and caress her head resting on my other arm. Her gaze searches my face before she sighs deeply.

"I'm sorry I lied about screwing another guy."

"Why did you say that anyway?"

"I still get mad sometimes about you and Kim," she says, wrapping one of her legs over mine. "I also get mad I'm with you since I promised myself I'd never forgive you."

"I don't care if you get angry and say mean shit. If you stay with me, we'll work through your resentment and distrust. Nothing else matters. I need my family. I refuse to spend another night alone."

Ruby's smiling lips kiss my chest. "One day, I'll lose the last part of my bitterness and truly forgive you. I wish I could snap my fingers and do it now. So far, that hasn't happened yet, no matter how many times I've tried."

"No hurry. You love me, and we're building a family together. That's all I care about. This right here with you and knowing Chevelle is safe and happy, that's what I need."

"And the Common Bend job."

"Yeah," I say, rolling to my side, so I can wrap her in my arms. "I know you think I'm a fool or reckless or an asshole. Whatever you think, I hope you understand why I need to be more than just an average Joe. All these years surrounded by people like the twins and knowing the power the Hallsteads wield, I felt like a loser not living up to the family name. When the Common Bend idea came to me, I knew it was my path. Until you gave me a chance and I tasted your lips again, I was too damn scared to make a move."

"I *do* have amazing lips."

"Fuck yeah," I say, kissing her tenderly. "I'd fuck you so hard right now just to make a point, but I think you actually broke my dick."

"Don't blame me. That was all you, buddy."

Smiling, I slap her butt and then roll her off me. "I'm fucking hungry. If I don't get food soon, I'll eat you."

Ruby tries to keep me in bed, even if I doubt she could handle me going down on her so soon. I tug her out of bed and slide one of my T-shirts over her head.

"I'm not cooking," she says while I lead her into the living room. "Also, nice butt."

Glancing back at Ruby, I wink and shake my ass for her.

"I can see why the ladies tipped so well," she says, opening the freezer. "There's nothing here. I think I have stuff for sandwiches."

"If you make me one, I'll give you a show."

Ruby's eyes widen, and she looks over my naked body. I turn slowly for her inspection, inspiring an impressed smile to warm her beautiful face. Unlike with the women at the parties, I enjoy when Ruby looks at me like a piece of meat.

"Deal?" I ask, stretching for her.

When Ruby nods, I already know she'll drool on my sandwich. Somehow, while staring at me, she manages to put together our food. She carries the plates to the couch, where she digs through her purse for dollar bills.

"Funny," I say, sitting next to her.

Ruby laughs at my expression and sits down. Wincing in pain, she loses her laughter but not her smile.

"My poor pussy," she whispers.

I cup her cheek. "When you make that pained face, I feel like a fucking king for knowing I fucked you right."

Smiling, Ruby reaches out and gives my abused cock a quick squeeze. I groan and flinch away.

Ruby smiles wider. "When you make that face, I feel like a fucking queen for making your dick my jester."

"I love you more than life," I say, meaning every word.

Ruby's smile falters a moment before she reaches over for a purple fleece blanket.

"I love you enough to let you eat in peace," she says, covering my lap. "And to stop ogling you for a bit."

"Ogle all you want."

As Ruby's gaze studies my face, I'm certain she'll cry. Instead, she nuzzles my bare arm and hands me the remote.

"The man of the house gets to choose what we watch."

Another small gesture to let me know she's working through her resentments and healing from past hurts. Tonight, we talk and eat like we did as teenagers on a date. Then, when our bodies are rested, Ruby and I return to the bedroom, where we fuck like rabbits like we also did as teenagers.

FORTY EIGHT - RUBY

For the second evening, Bonn works late, organizing his office. While I offered to help him, he swore I had enough on my plate with the new restaurant. I nodded at his comment, and he smiled at how I pretended to believe him. We both know he doesn't want me seen at his office, thus placing a target on my back.

With Camden hanging out with his club at Salty Peanuts, I decide to chill with Daisy at her condo. Elle finishes her homework quickly, so she can go to the nearby park. Soon, Daisy and I sit on a bench and watch my baby swing alone, even with children playing nearby.

"She doesn't like many kids," I say, sipping ice tea. "I used to think they didn't like her, and she was left out, but I was wrong. She is just picky about who she plays with."

"Like her mama."

"Yeah, I guess. It's why I don't have girlfriends. No one can compete with my sisters."

Daisy smiles, even though she's been in a weird mood since we arrived.

"Are things cool with you and Camden?" I ask.

"Yeah. He's great, and I'm great when I'm with him. It's better than I dreamed, and I had pretty big fantasies."

Nodding, I go along with her comment, much like I did with Bonn's lie earlier. *When did I become so fake agreeable?*

"Are you mad at me?" Daisy asks, startling me after we've sat in silence for nearly ten minutes.

"Of course not. Why, did you do something I should be angry about?"

"No."

"You wouldn't lie about that, would you?"

"No."

"Middle children are the worst," I mutter, fighting a grin.

"You don't call me as much lately," Daisy says, ignoring my teasing. "I didn't even know about your trip until Harmony said something."

Shrugging, I avoid her gaze. "Things are different now."

"Because of Cam and Bonn."

"Partly."

"But you were pulling away even before the trip."

Daisy seems younger than usual. Her insecurity has thrown her into little sister mode.

"If I tell you, you'll get upset, and I don't want that."

"I'm a big girl. Feel free to be brutally honest."

Watching Elle swing alone, I realize we both keep things to ourselves when in doubt.

"Since you fell in love with Camden, you've been annoying," I admit.

The corners of Daisy's mouth turn downward immediately, and I think she might cry. "Annoying?"

"You're at that point in a relationship where love makes everything right. For someone bitter and alone like me, your happiness was annoying."

"I wasn't trying to get on your nerves."

"No one who falls in love wants to be annoying, but we always are. When I first hooked up with Bonn, I was annoying, too. You don't remember because it was so long ago, and you were too young to realize how obnoxious I was being."

Daisy gives me a pouty look, and I wish I'd kept my mouth shut.

"Even though you hurt my feelings by telling the truth," she mumbles, "I still think you should have told me sooner."

"I know, but you were so happy. I didn't want to crap on your joy just because I was bitter."

"Well, you're happy now."

"It's not the same."

Daisy frowns. "We both have men who fucked up before we gave them second chances. Now, we're in love."

"On paper, it's the same. But Camden only started a stupid rumor about you. And the other people dumb enough to believe the idiot rumor were morons. Even when he siphoned your gas tank, he gave you a twenty to make up for it. Bonn cheated on me with a skank while I was nine months pregnant with our baby. So, yeah, not the same."

Daisy cocks an eyebrow. "Camden hurt me, and Bonn hurt you. It's not a contest."

"If it was, I'd win."

"Probably, but I can't be sure. Let's ask Harmony."

"Such a middle child," I tease.

Daisy flips her dark hair over her shoulder and gives me a dismissive eye roll. "You're competitive like all firstborn losers. Talk about annoying."

I imitate her pouty sad look and whine, "You think I'm annoying?"

"Love has made you rude. I blame Bonn."

"That's not the love, but you can still blame him. Great sex turned me into an obnoxious jerk."

"So very obnoxious."

"Are we okay?" I ask, wrapping an arm around her shoulders.

"No. You're hiding things from me."

"Is that what's really bothering you, or are you just pissed that I'm not hiding things from Harmony?"

"Well, there's that."

"She isn't connected to everything, and she's also around me more. If I hide something, she wears me down until I spill."

"I guess I could move back into my trailer. Has it been rented yet?"

Grinning, I hug her tighter. "Yes, and I don't think the new cat lady would appreciate the old one pushing her out."

While Daisy gives me a dark glare about the cat lady thing, I only watch Elle swing higher. My baby is fearless when she wants to be.

"Where are you and Bonn going to live now that you're back together?"

"I don't know."

"Really, or are you hiding the truth from me again?"

"Bonn is talking about finding a house for the three of us, but I'm not sure I'm ready for that step."

"Why not?"

Removing my arm from around her shoulders, I shrug. "We just got back together. Shouldn't we date and get to know each other a bit more before we move?"

"What's there to know? You haven't changed much since you were eighteen. He's a man, and they don't change much at all."

"Stop rushing me to pair up, just so you'll have a couple to hang out with."

"I'm not doing any such thing," Daisy lies.

"Uh-huh. Admit it. Being a couple makes it harder for you to hang out with Harmony and me. If you hook us up, we'll have more in common."

"No. That's not it, so shut up."

Daisy pretends to be angry at my accusations, but she's mostly pissed I caught onto her plan.

"I love Bonn, but I'm not ready to jump into house hunting and merging his crap with mine."

"You do love him, don't you?" she says, hugging me and refusing to let go. "I wanted you guys to get back together, but I never thought you would. Now, you have, and it's the best thing ever. Well, me being with Camden is the best, but you and Bonn are a close second."

Kissing her forehead, I smile at her enthusiasm. "It is pretty exciting now that I've gotten over the shock of him showing up out of the blue. And Elle is happier than I've ever seen her. Every morning when she wakes up and finds him at the trailer, she smiles like it's Christmas."

"You're going to make me cry."

"Oh, hell, you're not pregnant already, are you?"

"No. I mean, I hope not. Camden and I drink like a fish during the weekends, and I kind of enjoy being a lush right now. Adding a baby to our hedonistic ways already would be a downer."

I recall when I learned I was pregnant at eighteen. I'd been careful while taking an antibiotic and my birth control pill. We used condoms every single time, or so I swore to myself. *How could I be pregnant when I'd done everything right?* Except I probably did miss a condom once or twice, maybe more. I'd been young and stupid. Plus, Bonn was working in construction and often came over to my place sweaty. So, yeah, okay, I hadn't been so careful after all.

A baby wasn't convenient for my plans with Bonn. I imagined being my current age before we'd have our first kid. If I had gone to the clinic, things would have been easier, and Bonn wouldn't have cheated. Or maybe he would have cheated when we were twenty-six rather than back then.

But we never considered the clinic. I freaked out for two days about how my birth control let me down as if it were a self-aware entity out to cause havoc. As soon as I got a grip, I started thinking names and wondering if our baby would have straight hair like Bonn and me or take after my father's Afro-Caribbean roots?

I'd taken to the idea of being a mom quickly. I have no doubt Daisy will, too, when the time comes. Our lives always revolved around family, and I can't imagine that ever changing.

FORTY NINE - BONN

The Common Bend Sheriff's Office is a decadent building with stone walkways and water fountains out front. I imagine the cops skimmed plenty of money from what the dealers and whores handed over for the Reapers.

Five years ago, this town reveled in a golden age of easy cash and no overlord interference. The former strongman sheriff did his job, and the Reapers never sent people to micromanage. Those days are long past, which is why I arrive unannounced at the office intending to make the new pecking order clear.

The receptionist gives me the once-over, finding me attractive enough to offer a smile didn't give the man she just helped.

"I'm here to see Sheriff Tiller."

"Oh, I'm sorry, sug, but he's in a meeting."

"That's okay. I want you to get up and tell him I'm here, and he'll make time for me."

Her eyes widen before flashing back and forth to see if I'm joking. "I can't interrupt his meeting."

"I'm sure you think you can't interrupt, but I promise you that you can. I should also mention if you don't interrupt, you'll need to find a new job. I don't know about you, but I hate job hunting."

"Um... who are you?"

"Bonn Fletcher. Now, go tell the sheriff I'm here. Be sure to mention how I'm already complaining about the wait."

The receptionist glances around, still waiting for someone to jump out and tell her it's a joke. When I tap my watch, she cautiously stands before taking slow, uncertain steps toward the back offices.

I wait at the counter, focused on where the receptionist disappeared. A feeling as if I'm being watched finally forces me to turn around, where I find a blushing blonde.

"I remember you," she whispers. "You danced at my friend's birthday party."

"Sorry, but I don't remember you, and there'll be no repeat performance. I quit my dancing job, so I could stalk blonde women and burn down their houses."

"What?"

"Which part confused you?" I ask, enjoying her shocked expression.

"You burn down houses?"

"No, probably not, but maybe. I mean, I haven't seen what happens when people piss me off by running their mouths. Now that you're testing my patience, we'll see if a fire ensues."

"I don't understand."

Leaning forward, I speak slowly, "I'm saying you need to go away and never talk to me again. Do you understand that?"

The blonde swallows hard. "You're an ass."

"Wait, are you challenging me? I'm new at this bad guy thing, so I want to make sure you're really a threat before I go and do something I can't undo. So, when you called me an ass, were you challenging me?"

The blonde looks over at the uniformed officers at their desks. Maybe they'll save her, she thinks. Before she can find out, Sheriff Tiller appears from the back offices.

"Mister Fletcher," he says, holding out a hand long before reaching me.

After flashing a smile at the blonde, I shake the sheriff's hand and follow him to his office, where he shuts the door. I give the woman one last look before sitting down. I hope she runs to her friends and tells them how the stripper is a psycho. That way, none of them talk to me in the future. The last thing I need is them interfering with my new job or bothering me when I'm out with Ruby and Chevelle.

"How can I help you?" Tiller asks.

"You likely heard you have a new boss, and I'm his representative in Common Bend. Meaning if you have issues, you call me," I say, handing him a brand-new business card. "Mister Hayes won't hold anyone's hand in

184

Common Bend. He doesn't want to know about issues. If problems get so big that he hears about them, we'll both be in a world of pain."

"I don't want to seem ungrateful. However, what does Mister Hayes expect from my department?"

"You arrest who he wants to be arrested and look the other way when he wants you to. If he wants your men to have a presence somewhere, I'll let you know. Otherwise, you run the department the way any sheriff would. Protect and serve."

Tiller nods, but he's nervous. I see the sweat on his wrinkled brow and at the back of his neck. He's an average man in a seemingly average town now run by a not very average asshole named Hayes.

"In the past, you worked for an out-of-town boss," I continue. "The Reapers didn't care about Common Bend except for the profits it brought them. Mister Hayes wants this town to be quiet and well-behaved. I'm sure you want the same thing for the people living here."

"That I do."

"Then, we shouldn't have any issues. You do your job, and I'll do mine. If you need assistance, I have a local office. If I need your assistance, you'll do as you're told. Everyone is happy. No one needs to die."

Tiller looks as serene as a babe until my last sentence. I figured he needed reminding that Hayes didn't get to be top dog in White Horse without burying plenty of bodies on his way up.

Sure, I'd like to avoid bloodshed on my way to controlling this town. However, having made a deal with the devil, so to speak, I'll do anything to create a good life for my family.

FIFTY - RUBY

Bonn struts like a big shit when we meet a realtor named Sherry at a house in Common Bend. Shuffling along rather than strutting, I'm not thrilled with how quickly everything is happening. One day, I hate Bonn. The next day, we're looking for a place to live as a family. *When the hell did everything get thrown into fast-forward in my life?* Oh, yeah, the day Bonn showed up at the trailer and bullied me into a movie night.

"This house is in a great school district," Sherry announces while unlocking the front door. "And the yard is fenced like you asked."

The realtor barely acknowledges me. She's all about pleasing her hunky client. I follow them inside the house, where she talks about the refinished floors and high living room ceiling. Despite the house's appeal, I'm blind to the details. All I know is things are moving too fast, and I can't move to Common Bend.

"Can you leave us alone for a few minutes?" I ask the realtor, interrupting the rental's upgrades.

The woman doesn't immediately agree. First, she looks to Bonn to see if he'll ignore my request. When he gestures for her to go, she finally relents. I watch her hurry out and realize I'll need to get used to women fawning all over him.

I wait until the door shuts before I speak. Even with a moment to prepare, I'm startled by the emotion in my voice.

"This isn't happening. The moving and the changes, they're not happening. I don't care what that means, but it's what I want, and it's what will happen."

My words don't make a hell of a lot of sense, but I'm overwhelmed and struggling to keep my shit together. The last thing I want is to break down crying with the realtor outside.

"If you don't like this house, we can find another," Bonn says, caressing my cheek. "That's the point of looking at them."

186

"I know the point, and you know that's not what I'm talking about."

"You're assuming a lot if you think I know why you're upset. I really don't."

"You and I just went away for the weekend. We just slept together for the first time in eight years. We don't know what'll happen next, and you're already moving us into a house in a town where I don't know anyone."

"This house is less than ten minutes from Lush Gardens. It's not like we're moving to Nashville."

"I don't care. I'm not ready for this. Maybe you've spent years planning for us to get together, but I never thought we would. So, you showed up and pushed your way into a family movie and then dinner and then a kiss and then the laundry. Suddenly, we're going away for a weekend to act as a cover for you. Now, you want me to move. It's all happened so fast, and I'm not ready."

Bonn's face is a blank canvas, and I admire his ability to hide from me. He's tougher than I thought. That's good for his job. But right now, when I'm ready to burst into tears, I'd prefer he show me something.

"Tell me what you want," he asks, leaving the door open for me to say anything.

"I'm not sure. I spent every day hating you. If I didn't hate you, I'd crawl back to you. I thought I'd never forgive you, but I knew I would if we spent too much time together. I was right, of course. So, I have forgiven you, but I still don't feel it completely. I wake up wondering how I went from resenting you to sharing a bed. It's all too much."

"I still don't know what you want."

"I want to take things slower."

"Slower, how? Do you not want me to stay with you?" he asks, frowning as if I've lost my mind.

"Of course not. I want us to be together, but I can't make this big move to Common Bend."

"Where can we live, though?"

"Why can't we stay in Hickory Creek?"

"Because I work for Hayes, and my job is in this town."

"So? People commute. If there's an emergency, you're minutes away. Why can't you still live in our hometown where I feel comfortable?"

"It's just not done."

"Who makes those rules?" I ask, and my pouty Bonn shrugs. "Well, fuck them. We should make the rules in our life. Do you think if Hayes wanted to move next door to White Horse that he couldn't? Or if Camden decided to buy a house in Common Bend, that someone would interfere? No, they'd do what they want because they take what they want. That's supposed to be you, too. Isn't that what you did with me? Well, do that with our home."

"Is this because you're afraid to leave Lush Gardens?"

"Yes and no. It's my home, and I'm still freaking out about Daisy no longer living across the walkway. I feel like she's a million miles away. The trailer park is my security blanket."

"And that's where you want to live?"

"If you'd agree. I mean, I want to live with you, and there's no reason to waste money on two rents."

Bonn grudgingly agrees. "We can't stay there forever."

"I know."

"This is what you need, right? It's not me that's the problem but the location. I need you to be square with me."

Staring into his eyes, I say the words, "I don't trust you. I want to, and I know I should trust you, but I still don't. For so long, it's been drummed into my head that you're the enemy, and I still forget like the day by the pond. I'm trying, but I need time."

"I'm not blind, you know? I see how I've pushed things fast. I think I'm worried if I slow down, I'll lose everything. You and this job. Yeah, that's coming off like a pushy asshole, but I'll never get another chance at things."

"I know, and I'm proud of you, even if I'm pushing back at you right now. It's not about you, but about me and my fears and my weaknesses. All those years hating you filled a part of me. Now, that part is empty, and I feel scared. Like I blinked, and my entire life changed in an instant. First, when you cheated. Then, when you showed up at the trailer

188

and asked to go to a movie. So, I'm with you completely, even if I seem to be going in the opposite direction."

"With me forever, through thick and thin, right?"

"Through morning breath and bad jokes and blowout arguments over which Taylor was better in Duran Duran. I'm yours in every way, and we'll both have to get used to that fact."

A grinning Bonn is dying to defend his preferred Taylor, but he keeps his mouth shut by kissing me. Wrapping me in his arms, he looks around the house.

"It's a nice place."

"Yes, it is."

"I want to give you a home like this one day."

"You will, but we don't need to rush. Let yourself focus on your new job. We also need to get used to being a threesome. Elle says she loves having us together, but she's only known going back and forth all these years. We'll see how she feels when she gets no break from me," I say and then mutter, "Or you. Wanna bet she gets sick of me first?"

"Don't be so sure. She got homesick a lot. When she woke up from a bad dream, she asked for you."

"Really?"

"Yes. I'd show her pictures of you until she relaxed."

Tearing up, I smile. "You can't know how much that means for me to hear."

"I'm sorry I overwhelmed you."

"I'm sorry I'm having trouble dreaming as big as you."

"How about I work on slowing down while you work on dreaming bigger?"

Even nodding in agreement, I don't feel ready to think any bigger than Bonn, Elle, and me together at Lush Gardens. Between working on the restaurant and Bonn's plans with Hayes, I'm overwhelmed and would prefer to hide in my little trailer where time seems to stand still.

FIFTY ONE - BONN

After Clara Hallstead's marriage to Mojo Rutgers went down in flames, she hooked up with a former Special Forces badass. They had a son named Hudson, who likes to shoot things and study people as if wondering the quickest ways to kill them.

On the back of her property, her new husband, Erik, set up a shooting range. He also put together various obstacle courses, so their boy could grow up to be a better badass.

Over the years, Camden and Dayton invited me to their mom's place for shooting practice. I wasn't great with a gun, but I could hit someone dead square in the center mass.

"You'll die in a zombie apocalypse," Dayton warns me while lying in the grass nearby. "Probably best to die early on since you lack a killer instinct."

"Big talk from a man who missed the target," I grumble, throwing him a dirty look.

Hiding behind his mirrored glasses and under a ball cap, Dayton shows no reaction. I suspect his eyes are closed.

"Drunk-ass aim is what's ailing him," Camden says and fires at his target. "I don't think I've seen him sober in a month."

When Dayton doesn't react, we assume he's asleep and redirect the conversation.

"How's marriage treating you?" I ask Camden while sixteen-year-old Hudson ignores us and practices his already perfect aim.

"Daisy's got me on a diet. I'm eating healthy, no longer drinking alcohol, and even sleeping more. She's been a helluva good influence on me."

"Really?" I ask since he's downed two beers since we got here.

"No," Camden says, grinning as he takes a shot and misses. "Poor Bourbon Babe hasn't stood a chance against my bad influence. I have her drinking more, eating more, sleeping late on the weekends, and don't even get me started on the dirty games we play."

"If she's happy, I'm sure it's fine."

"You sound like Ruby. I forgot how you act when she holds your balls in her grip."

"I dare you to say that to her face," I taunt, smirking at the thought of Ruby nailing him in the crotch.

Camden shakes his head. "I still can't believe she's working for my mom. The entire pissing match between my parents boggles my fucking mind."

"People often forget that about Hickory Creek. The Brotherhood's got the tats and the muscles, and they make a lot of noise on their Harleys, but the Hallsteads run this town, too," I say, hitting another target in the chest. "You piss them off, and there'll be hell to pay. Your dad just got a refresher course on that fact."

"Your dad, too. You don't think my new cousin got the idea to play with matches around De Campo's on his own, do you?"

"I never considered much about it."

"You should. Rumor has it JJ was seen sniffing around the new restaurant."

My finger lingers on the trigger. Camden's words hint at a threat from a man who is my brother by blood and a dangerous stranger in every other way.

"Is there talk of JJ getting patched into the club?" I ask.

"Why, are you thinking of killing him and want to know if it'll cause a war?" Camden says, trying not to laugh.

"If I kill him, you'll never know it was me."

"Good point. His list of enemies grows every day. Hell, last week, he was making googly eyes at Rat's old lady. When he got called on it, he claimed he'd never want such a chunky bitch. Let's say that didn't go over well with the club, even if Howler tried to blow it off as a joke."

"What's Howler's deal with JJ?"

Camden shrugs. "He's old and losing his fucking mind. That's my theory anyway."

"He's not that old."

191

Camden glances back at his sleeping brother, who doesn't stir. "Howler and Mojo called a club meeting the other day. Then, they canceled it at the last minute and claimed they meant to have a club party. It was weird."

"They've pissed off people who are now hitting them back. It's likely happened before, and it'll no doubt happen again. I bet it even happens when you're running shit in the future."

"Sounds simple, but my mom's never taken on the Brotherhood in such an obvious way. Like, why make such a big deal out of a pizza place that I doubt she ever stepped foot inside?"

"She told the Brotherhood to leave the place alone," Hudson says, startling me since he hadn't spoken in over an hour. "They burned it down. What's so complicated?"

"If she has concerns, she ought to bring them to the club, not go behind our back," Camden explains to Hudson.

"Did you tell her that?"

The brothers share a steely glare, somehow on two sides of a fight neither started. Dayton turns over on the ground and finds another position. His disturbed sleep is enough to distract Camden and Hudson from their brotherly irritation.

Taking a shot and hitting the target's chest, I sigh. "Things are changing around here. Better to have it happen before you take over for Mojo, right?"

"No telling how things will be in ten years. Who will run what and what alliances will remain?"

"If you're looking for reassurance, keep looking. I don't know what I'm doing next month, let alone in a year."

"I never took you as a spontaneous asshole."

"Well, then you weren't fucking paying the fuck attention, fucker."

Camden laughs loudly, nearly waking Dayton. "Listen to that filthy mouth. You've clearly spent too much time around Hayes. I hope Ruby shoves a bar of soap in your mouth."

"Is that one of the kinky things you taught Daisy?"

Camden shakes his beer and tries to douse me with the squirting suds, but I'm already on the run. He chases me for

192

a few minutes. Unfortunately, he's slowed down after eating junk food, drinking lots of booze, and sleeping at odd hours. I laugh at him from a safe distance while he catches his breath and tosses the bottle in my direction.

While I don't know if we'll always be friends, I can hope I'll always remain a few steps ahead of him.

FIFTY TWO - RUBY

Our weekly karaoke night hasn't held up well since Daisy moved to the condo. We used to get together every Friday while the kids stayed with Mom. Nowadays, we're lucky to get Daisy for an hour before Camden starts texting questions. *When will she be done? Was she thinking of him? Should he order a corn beef or roast beef sandwich? Was she done yet?*

"He's a spoiled child," I tell Daisy when she checks her phone again.

"We're newlyweds."

"What did I tell you about being annoying?"

Daisy waves off my attitude. "I can't control whether he misses me or not."

"Whatever. Let's make drinks and start singing before he shows up wanting you to change his diaper."

Three peach mojitos later, Harmony sings "Time After Time" in her raspy voice. Depression clings to her, and I feel it infecting Daisy, too. If I weren't so tense lately, I'd likely be in tears by the end of the song.

"I warned you my song choices wouldn't be happy," Harmony says, resting her head against our sister's shoulder.

Daisy wraps an arm around her. "You sing whatever you feel like singing."

"I can't dig my way out of feeling like everything is doomed."

Daisy and I share a worried look. Harmony is always happy, sometimes overly so. Now, her depressed words set off every alarm. I don't know how to help her with her grief, but Daisy proves faster on the draw.

"Will Ruby singing 'Puttin' On the Ritz' improve your mood?" Daisy asks.

Harmony grins slightly. "Only if she dances, too."

Shaking my head, I frown at Daisy, but I'd never tell Harmony no. Besides, I don't hate the song nearly as much as my sisters.

I find a summer hat to help with my performance, really giving it all the pizzazz I can muster to make Harmony smile. My lame routine does the trick, and she's soon dancing with me.

When we catch Daisy messing with her phone—and likely answering Camden—we force her to join us.

"Enough of him for at least an hour."

Daisy nods, but it takes the "Safety Dance" to get her mind off Camden for even five seconds. We follow up the song with "You Spin Me Round (Like a Record)," ensuring Harmony will sing at the top of her lungs. The girl has no filter when she hears a certain tune.

We're on our third replay of the song when I hear a knock and nearly tumble in surprise.

"Who could it be?" Daisy asks, feeling paranoid.

Everyone in Lush Gardens knows not to disturb karaoke night. I grab my broom as a weapon and gesture for Harmony to answer. She opens the door, startling Camden and Bonn, who stand outside.

"What the hell?" Camden asks.

"Stalker!" I cry and try to shut the door on him.

Daisy uses her body to keep the door open. "What are you doing?" she mutters, stepping out of the trailer to prevent Camden from entering.

"What are you hiding in there?" he asks, trying to see inside.

"We're having karaoke night. Are you accusing me of lying?"

"No, but you're acting suspicious, and I thought you might have something going on. Let me look around and…"

"No."

"Why?"

Bonn rolls his eyes and asks, "Ruby, can I speak to you inside?"

Nodding, I watch him push past a grumpy Camden, who attempts to break down Daisy's defenses by tickling her.

Bonn enters the trailer and walks to our bedroom before turning around and walking back outside.

Following him, I grumble, "What are you doing?"

195

"Checking for a man," he says and nudges Camden. "Place is clean. Your instincts are shit."

"You wanted to come, too."

"Because you said a man might be in my trailer near my woman. You didn't mention this knowledge was based on your gut instinct."

Camden shrugs. "Hey, what can I say? Harmony likes weird men, and she's vulnerable."

"She likes Dayton," Daisy points out.

"Like I said, she has bad taste."

"I'm right the fuck here, children," Harmony mutters, taking the broom from me and swiping at Camden.

"So, so vulnerable," he teases, dodging her first swing but not the second. "Ow."

"Go away and leave us alone," Harmony says, smacking him again. "I get three hours a week when my sisters belong to me. You will not steal that, Camden Cheesestick Rutgers."

Frowning at Daisy, Camden sighs. "You need to stop telling them everything."

"Never!" Daisy cries, running back into the trailer. "Now, away with you, stalker!"

Harmony follows Daisy, and I shake my head disapprovingly at the men. "You heard the crazy. Be gone."

Before I shut the door on them, Bonn leans in and gives me a long kiss full of tongue. His embrace makes clear what he plans to do to me later tonight.

By the time he leaves, I'm a mush of hormones and longing.

"Nope," Daisy says, looking for a new song. "I will not have you swooning over Bonn if I can't do the same for Camden."

"I promise nothing."

We sing a few more songs before Camden's rattling at the windows finally draws Daisy outside, where he corrals her to his car. I watch them act like two fools in love and wonder if I can do the same with Bonn. Except I realize he isn't outside with his cousin. I text him and learn he's hanging out at Mom's with Elle.

"Why are you staying at the trailer park?" Harmony asks when I plop down next to her on the couch.

"I'm not ready for more changes."

"That's a cop-out."

"Excuse me?" I balk, startled by her tone.

"You're giving yourself an out with Bonn. If things go south, you'll have everything else in order."

"Well, duh."

"But you'll never forgive him if you keep waiting for him to screw up again."

"Forgiveness needs to be earned."

"It's been eight years, and you let him back in your bed. I think you're past playing it safe."

"That's easy for you to say."

Harmony takes my hand. "I've never seen you be weak before, and I don't like the look on you."

"He showed up and changed everything. I need time."

"How much? Weeks, months, years?"

"I don't know," I mutter, unhappy to be the bad guy.

"I think you should leave the trailer park. Staying here isn't healthy when you want to build something new."

"I don't want to move to Common Bend."

"Who does? Why can't you move to his condo?"

"It's his place."

"It has laundry in the unit. Daisy is nearby, and Elle already knows the place. You'd be moving up without having to leave Hickory Creek."

Squeezing her hand, I sigh. "You sound like you've been thinking about this."

"Ever since your first date with Bonn, I've wondered where you'd live. I prepared myself for you to leave."

"If you don't want me to leave, why are you pushing me to go?"

"Because it's the right thing for you and Bonn and Elle. It'll hurt me, and I know Mom won't like having you gone, but you'll be with Daisy. You'll be close to the restaurant. And while I'll miss you, it'll be nice having you and Daisy in one place since I'm lazy about driving."

197

Staring at the wall, I don't care if what Harmony says is true. The idea of moving panics me. No amount of logic can override those fears.

"It's not unreasonable to be afraid," I tell Harmony.

"No, it's not. Bonn hurt you badly, and he could do it again. Or you two could be happy for the rest of your lives. There's no promise either way."

"Without a promise, I can't make a move."

"Even if you're not ready, you need to tell Bonn to keep his condo, and you want to move in. Push yourself to do it because you haven't pushed yourself in a long time."

"What about Kentucky?"

"Yeah, and wasn't that exciting?"

Nodding, I admit Harmony's right about my fears controlling me. Kentucky was fun, and I'd felt like a new person away from Lush Gardens. The thrill of a fresh beginning is something I crave, but I don't know if I'm truly ready to let go of the resentment I've held onto for so long.

FIFTY THREE - BONN

Ruby asks me to pick up a few things at the grocery store before coming home. Her request sends my dick into an erection, likely knowing I've won back the body it so desperately craves. I swear sharing a bed with Ruby every night causes me to walk around with a hard-on half the day.

By the time I finish shopping, the damn thing is back in neutral after I made many promises about what I'd ask Ruby to do to it tonight.

"Hold up, Bonn," I hear while walking to my SUV.

Recognizing the voice as belonging to Mojo Rutgers, I ignore him and keep walking. I hope he'll go away, but at the very least, he'll be forced to catch up. Unfortunately, he isn't alone.

My father looks smaller than I expect. Of course, I was twelve the last time I saw him up close like this. The man seemed huge and fearsome. Now, he's another hungover middle-aged man in an area where everyone his age drinks too much.

"Did your mom not teach you manners?" Howler asks.

"She taught me to treat people the way they treat me. That's why I was ignoring you."

"Burn," says a laughing Mojo while slapping his VP on the back.

Howler doesn't smile. Normally, everyone kisses his ass. First, because he was the only son of the local rich family. Then because he was the VP of a violent biker club. I suspect one day people will kiss his ass out of pity because he's old and pathetic.

"Did you want something?" I ask Mojo, who's still chuckling.

Howler's the one to answer. "Do you need to ask your boss before you talk to us? He can hold your fucking hand, so your panties stay dry."

"I sense you're upset about something. Would it be how De Campo's is now a family-friendly restaurant? Or is it

199

because Common Bend belongs to a guy who thinks you're called Howler because you cry like a baby after sex?"

Even irritated at me, Mojo laughs again. I sense he's more pissed at his VP than me.

Howler curls his upper lip and leans forward. "Common Bend is a rough fucking place, and Hayes doesn't give a shit about it. When things go south because he hired a pussy to do his dirty work, he'll cut your ass loose. Who do you think will run Common Bend, then?"

"My guess is Camden and Dayton unless the Brotherhood wants senior citizens in charge."

Mojo is officially no longer amused by me. I can't help smiling since these fuckers have spent a long damn time ignoring the fact I exist. Now, I haunt their damn nightmares. They're lucky I'm not jumping up and down, giggling in triumph.

"Do you think you're safe?" Howler asks, leaning even closer, so I can now see the lines around his eyes.

"Like I tell my dealers, no one's safe because everyone is replaceable."

Howler's hands grip into tights fists, but I don't brace for the hit. He doesn't have the balls to fuck with me. Mainly because he doesn't know who the fuck I am, meaning he's clueless about what I'm capable of. I could be the scariest bastard in the universe or a sniveling coward, but he can't chance attacking me and learning the answer the hard way.

So, Howler steps back and shrugs like he doesn't care.

"Saving face, huh?" I mock while crossing my arms.

"You need to watch yourself."

"Okay, Dad. Are we done?"

Howler looks me in the eyes, and I can't imagine what he's thinking. *Is he wondering why he never reached out to me all these years? Does he wish he talked my mother into an abortion?* His mind could be anywhere because he's as big a stranger to me as I am to him.

I'm a little disappointed when he walks away. I don't know what I hoped for when I realized we were finally coming face to face. As Mojo follows Howler and they ride off, I think back to Kirk Johansson in Kentucky. He warned me that nothing my father did would fix what he broke inside me. Whether I killed Howler or we became best friends, I'd still end up disappointed.

I decide to do what Kirk did and focus on what I have rather than what remains out of reach. While Ruby and Chevelle are real, my father is nothing more than the man who fucked my mother twenty-six years ago.

FIFTY FOUR - RUBY

With Elle at school and everyone else at work, I find myself alone in the trailer. Unable to stop thinking about Harmony's accusations, I need to prove my fears don't mean I'm weak.

Except Harmony isn't wrong. I *am* afraid of change. Not just leaving Lush Gardens, but I'm terrified to trust Bonn. He's different now, and I pretend that's enough. Every day, I lie to myself about how I've forgiven him.

Except how can I forgive his sin when I've spent years avoiding any thought about the day I found out Bonn cheated? I hid behind a wall of rage to ensure I could survive and raise our daughter born only a month after he betrayed me.

Alone in my trailer with no distractions, I feel the memories return about the darkest day of my life.

We were suffering through a heatwave, and I was fatter than ever. Sweaty and miserable, I spent my days waddling around my mom's trailer. Bonn was working at a hardware store, saving up for a deposit on a trailer for us. We weren't in the best place in our lives, but our future was planned out.

Once the baby was old enough, I'd get a job while Charlie babysat for me. Bonn and I would get married eventually, but I was more interested in living with him. I hated how he spent half of his time at his mom's apartment. We needed to get the grown-up part of our lives started.

No doubt, half of Hickory Creek knew about Bonn and Kim before he woke up from his bender. Lori from the coffee shop told Betty, who told Mom who took me aside and shared the bad news.

As sensitive as she tried to be and as much as my sisters consoled me, there was no fixing what Bonn did with Kim. I didn't want to believe what I heard, of course. Bonn was the only man I'd ever trusted. He loved me completely, through bad days and good. We'd been teenagers together, moody as all hell, yet never spent a full day apart. We argued occasionally, but we always made up by the end of the day. Bonn wasn't the kind of man to cheat. That kind of man was his father, and my Bonn refused to be like Howler Hallstead. I was certain the rumor was a lie.

Except a part of me knew it wasn't. Deep in my gut, where I sensed I was having a daughter before the ultrasound proved it and where I understood my father would never make peace with me before his death. That part of me knew I didn't need to talk to Bonn to feel the truth. I'd already heard it from my mom.

I remember staring at my tear-stained face in the mirror and hating the woman looking back at me. She was a hormonal mess with pimples and dark circles under her eyes. Her hair looked like shit, and she walked around in oversized clothes rather than maternity gear since it was cheaper. If she hadn't been such an ugly loser, would Bonn's dick have wanted someone else?

A little after two in the afternoon, Bonn showed up at the trailer, looking hungover and as if he'd puked his body weight the night before. Worst of all, he was still beautiful in a way I wasn't anymore. When I stepped out to speak to him, I actually understood why he wanted someone else. I'd let myself go while he remained as sexy as ever.

Things might have ended up differently if Bonn had spoken as soon as I joined him outside. I felt like a loser who drove my love to cheat because I'd gotten too fat. All morning, my heart wanted him to give me another chance.

But Bonn didn't speak up immediately. He stood there looking sick and miserable, leaving me time to visualize him with Kim. The image erased my sorrow and guilt long enough to allow my temper to take over.

Kim was the loser, not me. Bonn fucked a piece of shit, and that made him a loser, too. He wasn't good enough for me. I never would have cheated on him if he got fat or his skin broke out from hormones. I would have loved him even if he weren't the beautiful boy I first fell for. I'd have loved him forever, but he couldn't love me that way.

Once I started screaming at him, I couldn't stop. I called him every name I could think of and said he was no better than his shithead father. Bonn only stood there like a wall as if my rage bounced off him. I finally gave up yelling when my throat began hurting. My last words were, "I never want to see you again."

And I'd meant it, too.

The only way to keep from groveling to Bonn was by waking up every day with hate for him in my heart. If I relented even for a moment, my love for him would return, and I'd forgive him anything.

Now, after so many years, I can't let go of the hate. Even when I hold onto Bonn and dream of our future together, the old resentments linger.

Reliving how pathetic and alone I felt that day awakens the pain I'd learned to live with. I look around the trailer, wanting to find something to distract me, but it's too late.

Leaning against the fridge, I slide to the ground and let the sorrow and humiliation rise in me. I trusted Bonn completely, and he fucked someone else. I make myself imagine him with Kim. I've avoided those thoughts for years because I needed to be strong for my baby. Today, I make myself feel it all—the betrayal, longing, shock, and the sense I'd never be whole again.

I'm still on the ground long after my sobs end. My mind replays the hundreds of times I saw Bonn over the years. How I avoided him at all costs, knowing his power over me.

Had I been wrong to cut him loose? Did I deprive Bonn, Elle, and myself of a happy family because my pride got the best of me? Bonn was the one who betrayed me, but I realize I'm the one who kept me stuck for so long.

"What's wrong?" Bonn asks, kneeling next to me.

I look up, startled by his presence. With the sun lower in the sky, I wonder how long I've been lost in my head.

"Why didn't you say anything the day after you cheated with Kim?"

Bonn doesn't seem startled by my question. "Nothing I could say would fix what I did."

"You could have tried."

"I know, and I thought about that a lot afterward, but it was too late. You wouldn't talk to me, and I couldn't force you."

"Until the day you did force me," I say, wiping my eyes.

"I got sick of waiting for a magical fix to the problem. Besides, if Camden got his girl, I knew I could get mine."

"You're so competitive."

"No, but I knew you and I were meant to be together. He just had the hots for Daisy and managed to create his opportunity. I watched him force his way into her life until she never wanted to let him go. I couldn't see that and not make a move I ought to have made years ago. I finally said the things I should have said the day after I cheated. I might have needed to say I was sorry a million times before you forgave me, but I should have tried."

"Yes, you should have."

Bonn sits next to me on the ground. "I regret that every day."

"We could have found a way to be together years ago, but we didn't. Why were we so stupid?"

"You aren't stupid."

"I avoided you," I say, relieved to feel him against me.

"I hurt you."

"We were raising a daughter together, and I couldn't be in the same room with you."

"Because you knew I'd seduce you if you were anywhere near my powerful pull."

Grinning, despite my bad mood, I shake my head. "You're feeling like a real stud now, aren't you?"

Bonn shares my smile. "I won the heart of the only girl that matters, and I did it twice. Yeah, I feel like a fucking king."

I rest my head against his arm. "You stole my confidence back then, Bonn. For years, I've been faking like I'm strong, and that's why I'm scared to leave my comfort zone. If I hadn't been so overwhelmed, I don't think I'd have agreed to go to Kentucky. Deep inside, though, I had to know if we had a shot."

"I'm glad you did, but if you hadn't, I wouldn't have given up. There's only so long a man can wait, and I'd hit my limit."

Bonn adjusts, so my face rests against his chest while his arm wraps around the back of me. He's no longer the boy I loved. I see little differences around his eyes. Bonn is all grown up, and I wish we hadn't spent so many years apart. I'd have loved to see my Bonn grow into the man now holding me.

"Did you tell the condo manager that you're moving out?" I ask.

"Not yet. I've been too focused on Common Bend and us."

"I'm glad because I think we should move there. It won't be such a big change for Elle, and I'll have Daisy nearby. Even if it's not a huge shakeup, it's time for me to toughen up and leave Lush Gardens."

Bonn doesn't ask if I'm certain. While I'm no longer the girl he fell in love with, he still understands me well enough to know I'm ready for a new start. One we should have enjoyed years ago but only now embraced for ourselves.

FIFTY FIVE - BONN

My mother takes the cigarette carton and a bottle of vodka I bought her. I watch her pour a little booze into her coffee mug. My mother's addictions are as much a part of her as the lisp in her speech and the limp in her walk. I never knew the young woman she was before meeting Howler and having me. That version of her probably didn't smoke and drink like a bar whore, but she was long gone before I got to forming memories.

"Ruby and I are back together," I say, handing her a picture Chevelle drew for her grandmother.

Mom looks at the picture and smiles a little, but her mind is on the booze. She takes a few sips before reacting to my comment.

"I'm happy for you."

"We're moving to my condo next week."

"That's a step up from the trailer park."

Sighing, I kneel next to her chair. "Is there anything you need?"

"I have everything. Thank you," she says, patting my cheek before focusing on the forever-playing TV.

Leaving her apartment, I think back to the melancholy I waded through all my life. Mom never broke free, and I used to worry I'd get stuck, too. Meeting Ruby gave me a way out. Even after I lost her, I had Chevelle plus the hope of winning back Ruby. Now, I'm free even if my mother never will be.

I'm desperate to get back to the trailer to enjoy my blessings and let go of my mother's unhappiness. I'll make popcorn and watch TV until Chevelle's bedtime. Afterward, I'll make Ruby come so hard she forgets her name.

"So, we finally meet," says a voice from behind me.

I decide to keep walking, forcing the guy to run to get in front of me.

"I'm in a hurry," I say to my half-brother, JJ.

"Oh, I bet you are. Making big moves these days, huh?"

Not giving JJ any more love than I offered Howler, I ask, "Do I know you?"

"I'd be surprised if you didn't."

"Well, then, color me the fuck surprised."

JJ shifts from one foot to the other, trying to hide his agitation. "Didn't anyone tell you that you had a brother in town?"

"I probably have a lot of brothers in town. Sisters too. Howler's dick leaked its way through most of the women in the northern part of the state."

"I guess that's right," JJ says, rubbing at his chin. "I still think you know who I am."

"Camden and Dayton mentioned Howler was big on playing daddy lately. So, yeah, I heard that much about you."

"Do I hear a hint of jealousy?"

Smiling, I shove my hands in my pockets and give him an "aw shucks" look. He's two or three inches smaller than me. Beefy up top but not so much from the waist down.

"Look, I get you're happy to have a dad in your life," I say. "It's every bastard's dream to hook up with their wayward parent and pretend as if they were always cherished. We all go through the Hallmark card dream, but I'll give you a little advice. You know, brother to brother."

"What's that, man with a plan?"

"Howler is at the midlife crisis age. Most guys will go wild and buy a Harley, fuck barely legal women, and play the tough guy. Of course, that's been Howler's life since he was old enough to get a hard-on. So, for a man like him, he'll go a different route and play the family man. Lucky for him, one of his bastards showed up looking for a hug. Everything worked out perfect for the asshole as usual."

"So, what's the warning?"

"A midlife crisis doesn't last forever. Sooner or later, an average man wants to return to his average wife and kids, sell his Harley, and stop pretending to be anything except a middle-aged square. In Howler's case, he'll tire of playing daddy and return to his life of not giving a shit about what his jizz created. When that day comes, you better hope you've made more friends than enemies in Hickory Creek."

"Should I consider you an enemy?"

"Man, my days of dreaming of having a brother are long gone, so I don't care if you live or die."

"You're the one who should be worried."

"Yet, I'm not, so what's that tell you?"

I step around him and keep walking to where my SUV is parked on the street. JJ follows at first, maybe thinking of starting trouble. When I don't take the bait, he turns and walks away. Sooner or later, someone will end him in this place, but it won't be me.

FIFTY SIX - RUBY

Sally and I sit on lawn chairs facing the community pond. To endure the dying heat of the day, we drink mint mojitos with lots of ice. Earlier, we packed most of my bedroom, and Bonn already moved several boxes of Chevelle's toys to his place. Daisy and Harmony plan to help me with the rest of the trailer. Soon, I'll leave behind Lush Gardens after calling it my home for over fifteen years.

"I should have planned for this day," Mom says, staring at the failing sun behind her gold sunglasses. "Nothing perfect lasts forever."

"What was perfect?"

"Having my girls and grandkids down the path where they could walk to my trailer whenever they wanted. For so long, I've had everyone I loved right here in Lush Gardens. Part of me thought I always would. Then, Daisy left and now you. Soon, Harmony will go. I'll be alone with Betty and Charlie."

"And Billy and the rest of the people here."

"Won't be the same."

Feeling guilty, I don't know what to say. My mother rarely gets depressed in front of us. Now, she's sad, and I'm the cause. *How do I fix her pain except to puss out on my plans?*

"Don't second guess yourself, Ruby," Mom says. "You're right to take a chance with Bonn."

"I still feel guilty for leaving."

"Don't. I never felt guilty when I followed my heart with silly men. We only have one life, and I don't want you to suffer from regret," she says, reaching out for my hand and giving it a squeeze. "Grab what you want and hope for the best. Sometimes, it works out like with Daisy. Sometimes, it doesn't like with my love life."

"You could try to find someone new."

Sally shakes her head. "No, I loved your father, who charmed me with his sweet words. Then, I loved a man completely lacking in charm. Finally, I went wild with a pretty man I could barely understand. In each case, I came out of the relationship with a bruised heart and a precious daughter. Now, I have a comfortable life in Lush Gardens, and this chance with La Famiglia Adding a man would do me no good. Long ago, Betty and I decided to be single together. Loving her doesn't leave me bruised, and my vibrator does the work she can't."

Laughing, I think about how much easier Mom's love life would be if she and Betty could get over their heterosexuality. Then again, adding romance to a friendship between two temperamental women might not be such a great idea.

After ridding myself of the visual of my mother and her pink vibrator she named Franco, I think about how much work is left at the trailer. Bonn's condo doesn't need any of my things to fill it up, but I'm still bringing as much of my crap as possible.

The reality of sleeping at the condo every night doesn't bother me as much as knowing I'll give up the trailer. Even loving Bonn and learning to trust him again, I crave a safety net if we fail again.

"Do you think Bonn will cheat again?" I ask Mom.

"I don't know. I've never understood men well. What do you think?"

"I think he believes he won't."

"Is there anything more he can do than plan to be faithful?"

"No, I guess not. As much as I want assurances, that ain't happening."

"You want to dream, but the last time you tried, life bit you in the ass. Just remember how he came back to you. I'd say he's worth the dream."

"I do love him so much, and I never could get him out of my system. That's probably my sign."

"Yes, and if things don't work out with Bonn, maybe you'll get another baby out of it."

Sally's expression sends me into giggles. Even knowing the hardships of raising children alone, she views my sisters and me as the consolation prizes of her failed love affairs.

I try to imagine returning to Lush Gardens with another kid in tow if Bonn and I crash and burn. Except my heart refuses to believe such a thing will happen. Though Mom never found a man worth keeping, I was lucky enough to find mine.

FIFTY SEVEN - RUBY

I can't deny Bonn's condo is addictive. At first, I was overwhelmed by the shiny newness of it. The entire kitchen reeks of excess. What in the hell do I need two ovens for? Embracing the decadence, I put a pizza in one and a pie in the other.

Then, there's the shiny shower and the big bathtub and the view and, of course, my beloved laundry room.

Unpacking most of my clothes, I plan to spend the evening in the condo while Elle sleeps at Mom's place. Each shirt I hang up in the oversized closet puts me in a giddy mood. By the time I dump my socks in his dresser, I'm bouncing and humming like a girl in love.

Bonn's mood sucks in comparison. After unpacking Elle's toys in her room, he sits on her bed for way too long. I peek in on him a few times before realizing he's lost in his unhappy thoughts.

I'm afraid to ask a question with an answer that could break my heart. Twice, I walk to the room before chickening out. Fear has owned me for too long when it comes to Bonn, so I force myself to speak.

"Are you having second thoughts about me moving in?"

Bonn looks up from his hands and frowns. "Never. Having you here is something I've spent many nights dreaming of in the dark."

"Really?" I ask, wondering if this conversation will lead to rolling around in his bed.

Bonn nods but makes no move to take our conversation to the bedroom. I feel him closed off to me and begin worrying again.

"You're making me nervous," I finally say when he remains quiet.

Bonn reaches over to caress my cheek. "There's work-related crap bugging me, but I don't know if I should get into the details. Camden claims he never tells Daisy anything about club business."

"Yes, but your right to keep me out of shit ended when you took Elle and me on a trip to biker heaven."

"True, but I don't want to burden you with my problems."

"If a problem belongs to you, it's mine, too. Besides, with our history, I don't think we ought to keep secrets."

"My truth is ugly. While I made the decision to do bad things to make a living, why should I corrupt you with my crap?"

"Stop protecting me and explain what's got you tied up inside." When Bonn still hesitates, I take his hand and play the Kim card. "The last time you held your problems inside, they ate you up until you made a mistake you couldn't undo. This time, you'll trust me with the ugly truth, and I'll help you through it. We'll face the problems together."

"I killed a man today."

Even suspecting his ugly truth might be like this, I still tense when he says the words. Bonn starts to pull his hand away and close himself off, but I won't let him go. Instead, I tighten my grip and make him walk to the couch.

"Tell me what happened," I say once we sit down, and I snuggle closer. "Your business is ugly, but I'm no wallflower. Talk to me."

Bonn studies my hand while running his fingers over my knuckles. "He was a dealer. The typical lowlife you think of when you imagine a meth dealer in a trailer park. Dirty and twitchy, and he knew what would happen if his numbers came up short. Some people always break the rules. They'll steal a pack of gum, just to steal. Lie about stupid stuff just to lie."

Bonn wraps an arm around me and rests my head against his chest. "When I was a kid, I felt like I did a good job protecting myself from the losers in my life. The neighbors were drunks or addicts. They were rude and violent. Everyone around me seemed rotten, but I kept my head down and stayed untouched by their crap. Through it all, I did watch them, and I learned what kind of people they were and how they viewed the world. The guy today was the same type of loser, and I knew he needed to go."

214

"So, you did the right thing."

"I knew if I let him pull his bullshit, other people would do the same. That would put everyone in danger in the long run. I did what I needed to do, but I don't feel like I expected I would. Guilty, you know?"

Bonn leans his head back on the couch. "Instead, I didn't feel anything. It was like when I was stripping, and I turned off a part of me and went through the motions. So, I'm bothered by not being bothered. Or I keep expecting it to hit me, and I get ready for the guilt or dark feelings, but they never come. What does that say about me?"

"That you know how to compartmentalize crap. It's how you dealt with your mom. You grew up alone with a depressed and disabled drunk. Yet, when we met, you never whined about it. That's your strength, but it's also your weakness. I think that's why you didn't know how to handle your fears about being a father. Normally, you'd shove those bad feelings away. That time, you couldn't. So, it built up until you freaked out. Now, you know you have that weakness, and you'll be smarter. But you also know you have the ability to do bad things to bad people without wallowing in guilt."

"Doesn't that make me a monster, though?"

"A monster doesn't love like you do, Bonn. A monster would never wonder if he was a monster for not feeling guilty. So, stop worrying. You were a damaged kid who learned to survive. A lot of kids in your situation might have grown up to be assholes, using their crappy childhoods as an excuse to treat others like shit. You didn't. You're a great father, and you treat me like a queen. Yes, you fucked up one time, but you won't again. We won't let you."

"You really believe that?" he asks, staring into my eyes.

"Right now, at this moment, I do. There will be times when I look at you and see the Bonn who hurt me. But it'll be your job to remind me of who you are now. Just like it's my job to help you when you get overwhelmed or need to vent. We're a good team. That's something I forgot all those years without you, but we complement each other. So, yes, I trust you not to fuck up. And you trust me with your work secrets. We'll make this work because the alternative isn't an option. We have to be together to be happy, so we'll face whatever we need to face."

I watch the confidence awaken in his dark eyes. I feel it inside me, too. This is us now—stronger, committed, and united no matter the obstacles.

FIFTY EIGHT — RUBY

Bonn wakes me up by yanking off the blankets and giving my bare ass a kiss. I gently swat him away, but his lust won't be denied. He lifts my left leg in the air and gives my pussy a leisurely morning kiss. There's no denying the man knows how to wake a girl in a good mood.

By the time Daisy texts to ask if we want to join Camden and her for breakfast, I've worked up an appetite riding Bonn's morning erection. We quickly shower and dress before finding Daisy and Camden making out in the hallway.

"Can we pick up Elle?" I ask, unsure if I want to spend an entire breakfast watching my sister suck on her husband's tongue.

Daisy needs me to ask twice before she can focus on something besides Camden's fingers playing with her hair.

"Oh, of course. I thought she was with you."

"No, she stayed with Mom last night, so we could move stuff in."

"Uh-huh," Camden says, walking toward the elevator. "I'm sure you worked hard last night."

A smiling Bonn gives my ass a quick pat but ignores his cousin's teasing. We take two cars, so we can move more boxes after breakfast. Even though Camden and Daisy leave first, Bonn gets us to Lush Gardens before them.

"Tonight will be the first time the three of us sleep at the condo," he says, reaching for my hand. "That's been a long-time dream for me. In fact, when I had a shit day or a grabby group of women while dancing, I would pretend you and Chevelle were in the condo with me. I'd imagine I tucked Chevelle in her bed and talked about school the next day. Then, I'd spend time with you before we went to bed. We'd talk about work. Though in my head, you were bartending again. By the time I'd imagine us in bed, I was relaxed and ready to sleep."

"That's the sweetest shit I've ever heard," I say, kissing his hand. "Funny enough, when I was tense, I would imagine you and me meeting in random places to have sex. We did it at the laundromat, Chevelle's school, at Sears. Oh, once we did it on the floor of the Boogie Bowl while people danced around us."

Bonn's expression is unreadable for a moment. Then, he adjusts his cock in his pants and shakes his head.

"You and I will continue this conversation later."

Smiling at the lust in his eyes, I'd love to work out some of his hunger in the back seat. Unfortunately, my horny sister and her hornier husband arrive to interrupt our horniness.

"Bummer," I mutter before reaching over and giving the thick lump in Bonn's pants a quick squeeze.

Now laughing at his expression, I hurry out of the SUV and join Daisy before Bonn can punish me for the raging hard-on in his too-tight pants.

"I know the feeling," Camden says upon seeing Bonn messing with his jeans.

Daisy gives me a triumphant smile before we walk from the park's lot to Mom's trailer.

"Now that we can double date," Camden says from behind us, "we ought to try out that oyster bar in Nashville. We might need to reserve two local hotel rooms just in case the urge overwhelms us, and we can't make it home."

"Ew," Daisy whispers over her shoulder.

"Being in love never means having to say 'ew,' Bourbon Babe."

"I don't think that's true."

"I bet Ruby wouldn't mind Bonn going wild on oysters and whiskey."

Before I can respond, my attention is drawn to Harmony's trailer, where the front door jiggles. We all stare as the knob turns, but the door doesn't open. I'm ready to ask Bonn and Camden to use their scary maleness to discover what's happening. Instead, the door pops open, and Dayton stumbles backward down the steps.

My breath catches, and Daisy grips my hand in surprise. We watch Dayton stare up into the trailer. A moment later, Harmony appears to tell him to be quiet. Her gaze leaves his face long enough to notice us watching them.

"So much for keeping things on the down-low," she mutters and then pushes him off her stoop. "Go away."

Dayton frowns as she shuts the door. Only after she locks it does he notice we're staring at him.

"She had a plumbing issue," he says, shrugging while fumbling with his shades.

"Is that what we're calling it now?" Camden asks.

Dayton shrugs again and walks past us. "Perverts think perverted shit."

Camden laughs first, followed by Bonn. The men look ready to chase after him and get the inside info. Maybe they figure Harmony will give up details easier because they let him go.

Daisy and I hurry to Harmony's door. We knock twice before she answers as if surprised by visitors.

"What?"

"Save the shit," I tell her while pushing my way into the trailer. "Why was Dayton here?"

"I was sad and drunk, and he was handsome and drunk. Let's not make anything of it."

Daisy opens her mouth to make something of it, but Harmony's expression shuts her up.

"Okay. Don't be so grumpy," Daisy says rather than going with the teasing she likely planned. "Want to join us for breakfast at IHOP?"

"Is Elle going? Can I bring Keanu?"

"Of course. We were heading to Mom's to pick up Elle. Get dressed and come along."

I know we won't get the specifics of Harmony's night with Dayton until she's worked them out herself. My youngest sister does things first and worries about the consequences afterward. Dayton ending up in her place overnight probably surprised her more than anyone.

Elle is wide-awake when we arrive at Sally's trailer. Keanu looks sleepier, but he gets his butt in gear once he knows we're heading out for breakfast. Soon, the seven of us gorge ourselves on pancakes while avoiding questions about Harmony's oops with Dayton.

For me, it's a perfect way to celebrate my last day living at Lush Gardens Trailer Park.

FIFTY NINE - BONN

My office is located between a nail salon and a used clothes store. My guys and I work on renovating the backroom and installing hidden compartments in the walls. We've finished with most of the work when the door's front bell rings. I peer around the corner to find my boss checking in on me.

In typical asshole fashion, Hayes doesn't call ahead. I like that quality about him. He knows to never give anyone a heads-up. I do the same with the dealers in Common Bend—show up randomly and say hi to keep them on their toes.

"Need something?" I ask, walking out to him.

"Are you having Ruby play assistant?"

"No, she already has a job. I hired a local girl with actual experience."

"Was that a fucking dig at my wife?" Hayes growls, once again challenging me.

"How do you mean?"

Hayes considers pushing the subject, and I wait for his next grumbly fuck you. Rather than play, he walks past me to where the guys work. Hayes gives the backroom a once over and then walks back to the front door.

"Kill anyone yet?" he asks.

"Sure did. Want the gory details?"

"No, champ."

I smile at his comment while scanning the road outside. "A dealer skimmed money off what he owned you. He also used half of his allotted product to throw a party for him and his friends. He seemed like a good candidate for me to use to scare the others."

Hayes follows my gaze and stares at the empty street. "Why this storefront?"

"It's close to the three locations where most of our distributors work. I wanted them to see me whenever they drove to the store or out to eat."

"You seem to have everything in order."

"I do."

"Can you see my fucking hesitation with trusting a former stripper with a multi-million-dollar investment?"

"If you want to micromanage, I can set up another desk here for you."

"Funny, asshole," he mutters, glaring at a passing man outside.

"Look, I've got things handled here, and I have Candy on speed dial. Anything else you want to know or see?"

"You're a smug fucker."

"It's better than being a stripper, wouldn't you agree?"

Hayes gives me a hard nod. "Tell me something, retired stripper. Was that the first person you've killed?"

"Yeah. Not a lot of killing opportunities in my old line of work."

"No, I wouldn't figure there would be," he says, crossing his massive arms. "So, how did it feel?"

I think about the gun in my hand when I made a visit to the guy's trailer. Rather than have him beg or try to change my mind, I shot him before he knew why I was there. Everything happened so quickly—entering his place to firing the weapon to wrapping his body to disposing of it deep in the woods. The entire event felt like a movie I was watching rather than a murder I orchestrated.

"I did what I needed to do to make a good life for my family. Anyone who interferes with their future needs to be eliminated. I don't have to enjoy it, but it needs to be done."

"From my experience, a man who enjoys killing won't take orders. Good to know you don't have a taste for it."

We share a moment of silence where we think about the lives we lead. The man I killed was someone's son. He also probably stole from his parents more than once over his life. *Was killing him okay because he was an asshole?*

Not in the normal world, but I wasn't playing by those rules anymore. The guy I killed wasn't any different than Hayes and me. He lived by the same rules. Breaking them, he chose to suffer the consequences. I didn't plan to follow his example. I'll be the most strait-laced criminal this area has ever seen. Hopefully, I'll live a long life doing what I once thought impossible for a nice guy like me.

And I'll do it all for my woman and our daughter.

EPILOGUE - RUBY

The first night we spend as a family in the condo, I start crying and can't stop for hours. I promise Elle that my tears are from lady issues. She looks at me with concern since she'll be a lady one day. I hug her tightly while we pray her hormonal crap takes a long time to kick in. I'd be happy if she were eighteen before she got her period.

Though I cry, I love living in the condo with Bonn. The place is beautiful, and every inch reminds me of him. Sitting on the soft leather couch with Elle on one side and Bonn on the other, I don't know if I've ever been happier. My tears are cathartic, helping me say goodbye to my safety blanket of the trailer park.

By the next day, I am completely on board with our new life. Waking up next to Bonn puts me in an amazing mood. We enjoy breakfast together with Elle before I drive her to school and head to the restaurant to check on the building progress.

La Famiglia will be open within a month, and I'm still thinking up a million ways to make it more family-friendly. So far, the Hallstead sisters love my ideas. They now rely on me more than Sally, who still can't take the plunge by quitting her current job. Taking charge, I choose chalkboard paint for the walls and relaxing Rockabye Baby covers of rock songs to play over the intercom.

The only time I hit a wall is when working on the website. Once the Hallstead sisters pay for a web designer, I become the idea woman while someone else does the heavy lifting.

Sally finally quits her job a week before our launch. I've already hired and trained staff while Chef Aaron has our menu down to an art. The plan is for me to open the restaurant and Mom to close. We have a few managers-in-training to pick up the hours we can't be there. Everything is falling into place. In fact, Aaron and I already consider adding catering to the business in six months.

Whenever work is stressful, I remind myself of home. Not in Lush Gardens but at the condo with Bonn and Elle. We fit together so perfectly as a family. I can't believe we ever survived apart.

I still fear someone will hurt Bonn. He's such a sweet guy with us that I have trouble thinking of him scaring anyone. He must be doing something right because Common Bend's flare-ups quiet until it's nearly as calm as White Horse.

Though Bonn doesn't want Elle and me visiting his office in Common Bend, we occasionally join him on trips to see Hayes in White Horse. Those visits are fun because we'll also go to the mall afterward. The downside is Elle somehow becomes tight with Candy's twins, Cricket and Chipper.

Now I'm stuck with having regular playdates with a woman I don't want to be friends with and who makes extremely clear she doesn't want to be friends with anyone. Then, fate intervenes when our pregnancies line up. She is miserable with Hayes's monster-sized baby while I end up on bed rest for high blood pressure. We talk all day, competing over which one of us is the most miserable. I never win, but I still like playing.

I guess I'm a late bloomer because I'm twenty-six when I finally get my happily ever after with a man I've known for over ten years. I have a dream job I didn't know I wanted. I make a friend after thinking only my sisters were worth my effort. For me, all the pieces fell into place after Bonn showed up at my trailer with a plan.

EPILOGUE — BONN

Ruby and I decide to let nature take its course with having a second child. We figure the sooner, the better since Elle is already nearing her ninth birthday. Once Ruby stops taking the pill, our son is conceived almost immediately.

We learn about her pregnancy a few weeks after returning from Dollywood on our first real family vacation. I feel like a fucking king being able to take Chevelle to the amusement park of her dreams. She brags so much to Chipper and Cricket when we return that they guilt Hayes into taking them. My badass boss refuses to get shown up by a former stripper.

Ruby's a picture of health and happiness until her fifth month, when her high blood pressure kicks in. Though I suspect she worries about a replay of my freak-out during her first pregnancy, she never mentions Kim.

Alone during the day, Ruby works online to get the restaurant's catering business started. Most days, I bring Chevelle home to find Ruby cooking us dinner. While she doesn't stay in bed as much as remain homebound, that's a big step for a woman unaccustomed to sitting on her butt all day.

The last two months are the toughest. Daisy and Harmony visit nearly daily to entertain her with gossip and karaoke. Sally comes over a few days a week to pamper her firstborn.

Remaining home with my woman as much as possible, I lie every day when Ruby asks if I miss sex. The lack of fucking and her weight gain leave her cranky. My solution is to dance naked in the evenings, usually to "Puttin' On The Ritz." Every single time, her mood improves.

"I need to get more dollar bills," she says while we cuddle in bed. "Do you want me to give you satisfaction?"

"Nope," I murmur, shooing her hand from my crotch. "If we get started, I'll want a taste, and we both know one lick won't be enough."

Every time we have this conversation, Ruby's expression reminds me that she misses sex as much as I do. *Talk about feeding a man's ego.*

Our son, Adric, doesn't look anything like Chevelle, surprising the hell out of me. His skin is darker, his hair straighter, his eyes more like mine than Ruby's. I'm fascinated by his handsome little face after nine months of imagining a male mini-Chevelle.

"Mine is cuter," Chevelle says, showing off the baby doll Ruby bought her. "Cries less, too."

"Chip and Cricket have been a bad influence on you."

Chevelle gives me a wonderful smile, but she isn't happy about her baby brother. Her jealousy takes us by surprise since she bounced for days after learning Ruby was pregnant. She was thrilled with being a sister until Adric first cried in the hospital. Chevelle backed away from him and has kept her distance ever since.

Ruby tells me not to worry. She was jealous of Daisy, who was, in turn, jealous of Harmony. Change is tricky, and Chevelle will like her brother more when he can do more than cry and poop.

By the time our energetic son is crawling, we're in the market for a new place. The condo went from spacious to cramped with the addition of a single tiny person.

"Babies need a lot of stuff," Ruby says, looking over the cluttered living room. "I guess I forgot that part."

We buy a three-bedroom stone-front ranch with a sizable backyard in the nicer end of Common Bend. Ruby and Chevelle bounce around the house once it's ours while I hold Adric and enjoy the show. They begin talking about getting a cat and a dog and maybe fish, too. We do eventually adopt a fat middle-aged cat from the shelter. Ruby can't believe Chevelle wants Biscuit, but our daughter falls hard for the chubby furball.

With our two kids, Ruby and I settle in for a quiet life. She works at the restaurant a few days a week and runs the catering business from home. I get to know so many people in Common Bend that I'm a town fixture long before buying into the zip code.

Occasionally during our busiest days, reality hits me on how much I've built in such a short time. How I took a movie night with Ruby and Chevelle and created my dream life. Everything I have is a million times better than what I imagined as a kid. I often wanted to be happy just to stick it to Howler. Now, I rarely think of him. My life is too big for such an insignificant fucker.

Sometimes when Ruby looks at me, I wonder if she's thinking about what I did and the time we lost. As if reading my mind, she always smiles like a woman in love. We might have taken a long damn time getting to where we were going, but the love of my life and I are finally here.

THE END

Printed in Dunstable, United Kingdom